\* \* \* \* \* \* \*

"You mean they write to men then marry them?" Susan said with surprise.

"Well, sort of," Martha said with a smile. "A girl will write to one of the men she has selected from a list we have of eligible men. If he writes back, they continue to write back and forth so they can get to know each other. If the girl finds a man she likes, and he likes her; the man may ask her to marry him. If she says yes, he will send money to pay for her to go out west to marry him."

"I don't know if I could marry a man I never met," Susan said.

"I think you would be surprised," Martha said with a smile.

\* \* \* \* \* \* \*

Other titles by J.E. Terrall

Western Short Stories
  The Old West
  The Frontier
  Untamed Land
  Tales from the Territory

Western Novels
  Conflict in Elkhorn Valley
  Lazy A Ranch
  (A Modern Western)
  The Story of Joshua Higgins

Romance Novels
  Balboa Rendezvous
  Sing for Me
  Return to Me
  Forever Yours

Mystery/Suspense/Thriller
  I Can See Clearly
  The Return Home
  The Inheritance
  Murder in the Backcountry

Nick McCord Mysteries
  Vol – 1 Murder at Gill's Point
  Vol – 2 Death of a Flower
  Vol – 3 A Dead Man's Treasure
  Vol – 4 Blackjack, A Game to Die For
  Vol – 5 Death on the Lakes
  Vol – 6 Secrets Can Get You Killed

Peter Blackstone Mysteries
  Murder in the Foothills
  Murder on the Crystal Blue
  Murder of My Love

Frank Tidsdale Mysteries
  Death by Design
  Death by Assassination

# THE VALLEY RANCH WAR

**by**
**J.E. Terrall**

*Best Wishes*
*J.E. Terrall*

Printed in the United States of America
First Printing / 2016 – www.createspace.com


Cover: Front and back covers by author, J.E. Terrall

Book Layout /
Formatting:    J.E. Terrall
               Custer, South Dakota

# THE VALLEY
# RANCH WAR

To
Mary Krogman,
friend and fellow historian

# CHAPTER ONE

Gray clouds hung low over the city after a brief morning shower. There was a slight chill in the air. Having just turned sixteen, Susan Farnsworth had to leave the orphanage. She gathered her meager belongs into two small carpetbags and a paper sack, took a deep breath, then she stepped out into a world that was unfamiliar to her. She looked back at the dull dingy building she had lived in for the past fourteen years.

Although the orphanage was not a place anyone would want to live, it was the only place Susan knew since she had been left there when she was only two years old. It was difficult being an orphan in the 1880's in Chicago.

Standing out in front of the orphanage, she looked up and down the street. She had no idea which way she should go. If she went to the right, she had no idea what might lie before her. For that matter, she had no idea what lie before her if she went to the left. She had never been very far from the orphanage in all the years she had lived there. In fact, she had never been more than a couple of blocks away from the building in any direction, and certainly never alone. It frightened her to know that she could not simply turn around and go back inside. For the first time she was all alone.

With no idea of where to go, she started walking down the street to her right. It was not that she had any idea what would be in her future down the street to her right, it was simply the way she turned.

Susan walked slowly down the sidewalk looking at each building on both sides of the street. They all seemed to look the same to her. She had no idea what she was looking for, but it seemed the natural thing for her to do. She had no idea where she was going, or what she might find in the next block, or the block after that, or the block after that. Susan had never felt so alone and so scared in all her life. She had always had the security of the orphanage.

Now that she was out of the orphanage and on her own, where was she going to live? How was she going to eat without any money? What was she going to have to do just to survive? There were no answers to all the questions racing through her head as she continued to walk along the sidewalk.

She had only gone about six or seven blocks when her feeling of hopelessness and fear over took her and filled her eyes with tears. Her eyes were so full of tears she had to stop because she could no longer see. She managed to wipe the tears from her eyes long enough to find the steps leading up to a building. She sat down on the steps and gathered her two small carpetbags and one paper sack tightly against her side as if they would protect her, then leaned against the railing along the steps and began to cry.

She was so frightened and so immersed in the hopelessness of her situation that she didn't hear the sounds of someone walking along the street. She didn't even hear the sound stop when it was very close to her.

"Excuse me," a woman said softly. "Are you all right?"

The sudden sound of a voice startled Susan. She quickly looked up as she drew back against the railing and began wiping the tears from her eyes. As soon as she could see, she looked up at the woman wondering who she was and what she wanted.

"I'm sorry to have frightened you, but you look like you are in need of help," the woman said, her voice soft and kind. "Are you in need of help?"

The woman looking down at Susan was young and very pretty, though several years older than Susan. She had beautiful brown eyes and dark brown hair that flowed gently out from under her bonnet. She was wearing a very nice dress, nothing like the dresses Susan had seen in the orphanage. The woman's dress looked very expensive. The woman looked at Susan as if she really was concerned about her.

Susan didn't know what to say to her. The woman was a stranger; and she had been taught not to talk to strangers, but she had to admit to herself that she really did need help. It seemed rude not to at least answer the woman's questions, especially if she might be able to help her.

"Yes, I am in need of help," Susan admitted shyly.

"Why don't you come with me? We can talk about it. Maybe I can help. My name is Martha McHarris. I live just a little way down the street," she said as she reached down to pick up Susan's carpetbags.

Susan hesitated to let her take the carpetbags because they contained everything she had in the world. She was not really sure she should go with this stranger, but what choice did she have if the woman could help her.

"Come with me," Martha said softly as she reached out a hand to Susan. "I'm sure I can help you."

Susan slowly smiled up at Martha, reached out and took her hand. Once she was on her feet, she let Martha pick up her two carpetbags. Susan picked up her sack and held it close to her slender body, then began walking beside Martha. Susan watched Martha wondering where she was taking her. It occurred to Susan that almost any place was better than the orphanage, and certainly better than sleeping out on the street.

"Are you from the orphanage?" Martha asked as they walked along the sidewalk.

"Yes," Susan replied. "How did you know?"

"I have seen many of the girls who are sent away from the orphanage at your age. They are not so different from you. I'm sure that I can help you. My husband and I have helped many young girls. I grew up in an orphanage, too; so I know what it is like. What is your name?"

For the first time she believed that the young woman would understand what she was going through, and decided she would answer her.

"Susan Farnsworth."

"That is a nice name," Martha said with a smile.

They hadn't gone very far when they turned in front of a large, very nice brick house. Susan stopped and looked up at the house. She had only seen houses like it in old magazines that had been donated to the orphanage for them to read, at least for those who had learned to read.

"It's all right. I live here," Martha said when Susan hesitated to start up the long walkway to the house.

Susan smiled at Martha, but the look on Susan's face was that of someone who was not sure it was a good idea. After all, she didn't know the woman. She took only a moment to decide because she had no other options. The idea of sleeping in the street frightened her more than going with Martha. She followed Martha up the steps.

Once inside the house, Susan looked around. The ceiling was high and ornately decorated with light colors of blue and cream between the large wooden beams. The sofa and chairs were covered in velvet with polished wood trim, something Susan had never seen before.

"Right this way," Martha said, then turned toward a spiral staircase.

Susan looked at her, then followed her up the long curved stairway to a room on the second floor. Martha opened the door to a room, then stepped back to permit Susan to enter.

"This will be your room for as long as you need it," Martha said, her voice pleasant and reassuring.

Susan stepped into the room and looked around. She had never seen a room so beautiful. Martha put Susan's carpetbags on the floor at the foot of the bed. Still clutching her paper sack, Susan sat down on the bed. It was not only a beautiful room, but the bed was far softer than those in the orphanage, and it even had clean sheets on it. The room smelled of fresh flowers.

"I'll be downstairs. Take your time to get settled in then come downstairs. We can talk when you are ready," Martha said with a smile, then turned and left Susan alone.

Susan took her time to look over the large room. On top of a dresser was a large beautifully decorated bowl with a matching pitcher and there was water in the pitcher. There were clean fresh towels on a bar on the side of the dresser. The cover on the bed even matched the real drapes over the windows. She had never seen a bedroom like it before.

As soon as she had gathered her thoughts, she straightened her simple cotton dress, left the room and went downstairs. At the bottom of the stairs she looked around, but didn't see anyone. However, she could hear people talking somewhere down a long hall. She followed the sounds of the voices until she came to a large room where there were ten other young ladies, most of them not more than a year or two older than her, and they were sitting on chairs in a circle.

"Please, come in," Martha said with a smile. "We have been talking about the letter Judy received today. You can sit over there."

Susan looked at Martha as if she didn't understand, but she moved across the room to the empty chair Martha had pointed to then sat down on it. She felt a little nervous not knowing anyone in the room, and they were all looking at her.

"Everyone, this is Susan," Martha said. "Like the rest of you, she is all alone."

They took a few minutes for the girls to introduce themselves before Martha interrupted them.

"I'm sorry. Let me explain what we do here. The young women here are alone in the world, just like you. My husband and I arrange for them to write to men who live in the west and are seeking a wife. There are very few women out west for men to marry, have a family and make a life together. The young women you see here are what we call mail order brides."

"You mean they write to men then marry them?" Susan said with surprise.

"Well, sort of," Martha said with a smile. "A girl will write to one of the men she has selected from a list we have of eligible men. If he writes back, they continue to write back and forth so they can get to know each other. If the girl finds a man she likes, and he likes her; the man may ask her to marry him. If she says yes, he will send money to pay for her to go out west to marry him."

"I don't know if I could marry a man I never met," Susan said.

"I think you would be surprised," Martha said with a smile. "Judy, would you like to read your letter?"

Susan listened while Judy read her letter aloud. The man who wrote the letter asked Judy to marry him. She seemed very excited. When she was finished reading the letter and looked at the other girls, Susan could see how excited they were for Judy. It was at that point Susan began to think about it.

"I'm going to my room and write to him," Judy said with a wide grin. "I'm going to tell him I would love to marry him."

After a short time of living and working in the home with the other girls and seeing the smiles and excitement of the girls who were asked for their hand in marriage, Susan told Martha she wanted to be a mail-order bride.

Within a day or so, she had picked out the name of a man and wrote to him. The name she had chosen was Jacob McDonald. It took almost three weeks before she got a return letter from Jacob. During that time, she wondered if he had not liked what she had written in her letter to him. She found out that Jacob McDonald lived in the Dakota Territory in an area known as the Black Hills. They began writing back and forth for almost a year before Jacob wrote and asked her to come to Custer City to marry him. In his letters, he had told about his ranch in the Black Hills, telling her how beautiful it was there in the mountain valley where his ranch was located.

Finally, the day came when his letter arrived asking her to marry him. He didn't promise her anything other than he would give her a home in a beautiful valley where he would do everything he could to make her happy. That was enough for Susan to accept his offer of marriage. She found herself as excited as Judy had been when she was asked to marry, but Susan was very nervous, too. She wrote back accepting his offer to marry him.

When she received his letter with the money to buy her tickets and pay for her meals along the way to Custer City, she immediately wrote to him and told him she would meet him in Custer City.

With the help of Martha and her husband, she made plans for the trip and got ready to leave Chicago. When the day arrived for her to leave for Custer City in the Dakota Territory, Susan went to the train station and was seen off on the journey of a lifetime by her now very good friend, Martha. She promised to write Martha and tell her about her new home.

Excited, but still rather nervous about the trip and what it would hold for her, she got on the train and began her journey west. With several delays and a number of changes from one train to another, she arrived at Sidney in Nebraska.

From there she took the Sidney to Deadwood stagecoach as far as Custer City where she was to meet Jacob face to face for the first time.

As the stagecoach rumbled over the trail to Custer City, many thoughts ran through Susan's mind. Had her decision to marry Jacob been the right decision? Was he really what he said he was? Was she making a big mistake by leaving Chicago for a place that she knew nothing about?

She had set out to start a new life while leaving the old one behind. It was scary, but she was leaving behind a life as uncertain as the one she was going to. That thought seemed to reassure her, at least a little.

# CHAPTER TWO

It was a hot early May afternoon in 1883 when the Sidney to Deadwood stagecoach arrived at the stage stop near the center of Custer City in the Dakota Territory. The driver yelled for the horses to stop as he pushed hard on the brake handle with his foot while pulling back on the reins. The stagecoach stopped in a cloud of dust in front of the stage stop. The driver wrapped the reins around the brake handle then climbed down from the stagecoach. He tied the lead horses to the hitching rail, then opened the door to let the passengers out of the stagecoach.

There were only four passengers on the stagecoach. One was a well-dressed man who looked like he might be a businessman. There was a young couple on their way to Deadwood, and Susan.

"This here's your stop, Missy," the driver said to Susan.

Susan moved to the door and looked out. She looked up and down the street. The street was very wide, and had deep ruts in it made by heavy freight wagons. She could see a freight wagon with four teams of oxen hitched to it in front of the freight office. A number of the buildings appeared to look new while some of them looked as if they had been there for a few years.

"You gettin' out Missy?" the driver asked disturbing her thoughts.

"Yes. Would you be so kind as to put my bags on the boardwalk?"

"Sure thing, Missy."

The driver took her carpetbags from the stagecoach and set them down on the boardwalk. He noticed she was looking the town over. From the look on her face, he thought she might be a bit disappointed in the town.

"It ain't much of a town, but it'll grow," the driver said as he reached out a hand to help her down.

Susan took his hand and stepped down from the stagecoach. She walked over to the boardwalk, then turned and looked around. Susan knew she was to meet Jacob at the stage stop, but she did not see him. With nothing else to do, and not knowing anyone who lived there, she sat down on a bench in front of a store and set her carpetbags next to her.

She began to think about what she had done to get to this little town in the middle of the Black Hills, and why she was there; then she began to wonder if it had been a good idea. It was at that moment she remembered something Martha had told her at the train station in Chicago. She smiled to herself.

"It is a new life you are going to that is no more uncertain than the one you are leaving," Martha had said.

The trip had given her a lot of time to think, but now she was really in Custer City where she was to be married to a man she had never met. She only knew about him from what he had told her in his letters and the picture he had sent her.

Susan sat on the bench looking around for the man she was there to marry, but he didn't seem to be anywhere in sight. She watched as the stagecoach left the stage stop and headed on to Deadwood. Since she didn't have a ticket to go any further, and she didn't have a ticket to return, there was nothing else for her but hope Jacob would show up before evening. She didn't know what she would do if he didn't come to get her. Even though she had spent the money she had been sent very carefully, she was sure she didn't have enough money for a room at the hotel for more than a night and for no more than one or two meals.

Her attention was suddenly drawn to the saddle shop across the street. A fairly tall man with a nice build stepped out of the shop and started across the street. Susan instantly recognized him from the picture he had sent her. He looked to be in his early thirties, some years older than her. He had a pleasant smile on his face as he walked across the street and stepped up on the boardwalk in front of her.

"Susan?" he asked smiling at her.

"Yes," she replied, shyly. "Jacob?"

"Yes. You are more beautiful than your picture."

Susan smiled at him. She didn't know what to say.

"I hope you are not disappointed in me," Jacob said.

"No. Of course not," she said with a shy smile.

"I have a room over at the hotel where you can freshen up a bit before we go to the church."

"That would be nice," she said. "Could we stop somewhere and get a cup of coffee? I would like to talk to you for a little while before we get married."

"Sure, of course," he said a little worried she might have changed her mind about marrying him now that she had a chance to see him in person.

"Let me help you with that," Jacob said as he reached out and picked up her carpetbags.

He then took her gently by the arm. He walked with her to the hotel where there was also a small dining room just off the lobby. After putting her carpetbags down next to a table, he pulled back a chair for her. He watched her as she sat down, then he sat across the table from her.

"What is it you would like to talk to me about? I know I have a lot to tell you," he said.

"Can you tell me about your ranch?"

"Well, like I said in my letters, it's a small ranch in a valley back in the Black Hills. I have built a cabin for us, and a barn for the horses, and I have fenced off some of the land to help keep the cattle from wondering off into the woods. I have a lot more to do, but I think you will find the valley a beautiful place to live. There is a lot of grass and a clear creek that runs the full length of the valley all year round. I built the cabin fairly close to the creek so you don't have to go very far for water. We will drill a well as soon as we can."

She couldn't help but notice everything he said he had done on the valley ranch had apparently been done with her in mind. It pleased her to think he built the place just for her.

"Are there any neighbors nearby?"

"Our closest neighbor is not a very friendly man. I don't think he has a wife. We don't get along very well," Jacob said hoping that it would not discourage her from marrying him. "But there is a very nice woman who lives at Four Mile Stage Stop. You will get a chance to meet her on our way to the ranch."

"How far is the stage stop from the ranch?"

"It's about a three-hour ride in the wagon, maybe a bit more."

"Oh," Susan said with a hint of disappointment. "Is there anyone else near your ranch?"

"No, I'm afraid not," he said worried that she might want to go back to Chicago.

Jacob sat and looked at Susan. From the expression on her face he thought that he probably should have told her more about how secluded the ranch was from the rest of the world. He was used to being alone, but he was sure that she was not since she was from Chicago.

Thinking she might have caused him to worry about her staying, Susan reached out and put her hand over his. When he looked up at her, she smiled and gently squeezed his hand.

"I'm not going back to Chicago. I would like to go to the room and freshen up a little before we go to the church," she said softly as she smiled at him.

"Of course," Jacob said as he stood up, feeling much better.

Jacob went to the desk clerk and got the key to the room. He carried her carpetbags up to the room and let her in.

"We will be staying here tonight, but right now I'll go wait for you in the lobby. Take your time. We don't have a set time to be at the church."

"Thank you," Susan said then watched him as he left the room.

She turned around and looked the room over before she walked to the washbowl, the pitcher of water, soap and towel on the table. She washed her face and arms then sat down on the edge of the bed.

She closed her eyes and thought about Jacob. His letters had been very nice, but more importantly he seemed like a nice person. Although she was a little nervous about marrying a man she hardly knew, she was sure they would be able to grow to love each other over time. That thought made her feel a little better about having accepted his proposal of marriage.

When she was ready, she took a deep breath then left the room to meet Jacob in the lobby. When she entered the lobby she found Jacob sitting in a chair. He stood up immediately when he saw her.

"You are beautiful," he said as he took her arm.

She simply smiled at him and let him lead her to the church. When they arrived at the church, they found the minister and his wife and another couple waiting for them. The wedding was rather simple and didn't really take very long. The minister presided over the ceremony while the minister's wife played a foot pump organ. The owner of the general store and his wife had come to the church to be witnesses to their wedding. After Jacob and Susan were married, they went back to the hotel where they had dinner then went to their room.

Jacob was very gentle with her. He turned his back while she got ready for bed. Once they were in bed, Jacob could see she was very nervous, and he didn't want to do anything to frighten her.

"I guess you had a pretty long trip, and you're probably tired. If you would like to go to sleep, I will understand."

"Maybe we could just lie close together tonight," she suggested.

"That would be nice. It is a long trip in a wagon to our ranch.

"Thank you," she said as she moved close to him.

He reached out to her and drew her close. He put his arm around her then laid quietly. It wasn't long and they were sleeping comfortably.

In the morning, Jacob got up and dressed while Susan remained in the bed. As soon as he was ready, he looked at Susan. He could hardly believe such a pretty young woman would really want to be with him.

"I'll go get the horses hooked up to the wagon, and meet you at the general store. I have to get a few things. There may be a few things you will need. You can get them there."

"Thank you. That would be nice. I'll try not to keep you waiting," Susan said as she smiled at him.

"We can get some breakfast at the café at the edge of town on our way out, if that's okay."

"That would be fine," she said then watched him leave the room.

Jacob went to the livery stable and harnessed the team of horses to his wagon. He took the wagon to the general store, tied the horses in front, then went inside to get his supplies. Susan did not keep him waiting. She was at the general store by the time he had arrived with the wagon.

Jacob purchased supplies and some cloth for Susan. She also got a few things like thread, pins and needles for sewing. As soon as they were done shopping, they went to the little café at the end of the street and had breakfast. After breakfast, they headed for the small valley ranch deep in a mountain valley in the western part of the Black Hills.

On their way to the valley ranch, Jacob and Susan stopped for a meal at the Four Mile Stage Stop. It gave Susan a chance to meet the owners and get acquainted with them. Susan and Jacob spent an hour or more eating a good meal and talking with Mary Miller and her husband, John. By the time Susan and Jacob had to leave to be able to get to the cabin before dark, Susan was sure she had found a friend in Mary.

They didn't stay long because it was still a long way to the ranch. Jacob bought a couple of bags of oats for the horses and loaded them into the wagon. He helped Susan get up on the wagon then got up beside her.

"I hope you come for a visit sometime after you get settled in," Mary said looking up at Susan.

"I would like that," Susan said.

"I'll bring her by for a visit," Jacob promised.

Jacob released the brake arm, slapped the horses on their rear with the reins and called out to them to move on. As the horses pulled the wagon on down the road, Susan looked back and waved at Mary and John.

After they were almost out of sight of the stage stop, Susan turned around and slipped her arm around Jacob's arm. She leaned against Jacob and watched the country as they moved along. Jacob looked at her and smiled.

It seemed like forever before Jacob turned off the road onto a narrow trail that wound through the thick forest. The horses continued to move along until they came to a narrow canyon that went deeper into the hills. Jacob turned the horses into the canyon. The horses didn't mind the narrow canyon. They had been through the canyon many times.

When Jacob drove the wagon out of the narrow canyon and into the valley, he stopped. He looked at Susan only to find her looking at him. The look on her face seemed to ask him why they had stopped.

"This is our ranch. What do think?" Jacob asked, a little worried about what she would think of it.

Susan took a moment to look around. The sun was getting ready to set, but it still lit up the valley. The ground was covered with thick green grass. Surrounding the valley was a thick forest of pine trees with gray rock ridges jutting out and reaching up to the clear blue sky above the ridges behind the trees. There was a creek that flowed slowly as it wondered down through the valley. She could see twenty-five or thirty cattle grazing peacefully off in the distance. She could also see a small cabin with a barn off to the right side of the valley. It wasn't a very big cabin, but it was big enough for the two of them, she thought.

Susan reached over and took his arm as she took in their ranch. She smiled then turned and looked at Jacob.

"It's the most beautiful place I have ever seen," she said as she smiled up at him.

"Do you think you could be happy here?" he asked nervously.

"I'm sure I will be," she said.

Jacob smiled then called out to the horses to move on as he slapped them on the rear with the reins. The horses pulled the wagon off across the valley toward the barn. When they reached the barn, Jacob got down off the wagon and helped Susan down.

Susan walked over to the cabin and pushed open the door. She stepped inside then stopped to look around. It wasn't a very big cabin, but it looked nice. On one end was a fireplace made of stone with a mantel above it. There was a small picture frame with a picture of her in it. A table and two chairs were only a few feet from the fireplace and there was a cupboard along the wall. Close to the cupboard was a dry sink in the corner. There were only two windows in the cabin, one on the front just to one side of the door, and one on the side that looked toward the barn. There was a bed opposite the fireplace with a handmade quilt and two pillows.

She had just finished looking over the cabin when Jacob came inside. He looked at her and wondered what she was thinking.

"It's very pretty here," she said.

"We can move any of the furniture around if you want it arranged a little differently," Jacob said.

"It will be fine," she said as she looked at him and smiled.

Jacob smiled at her, then retuned to the wagon. He gathered her belongings and took them into the cabin. He then went out to take care of the horses and the other supplies.

Susan spent the next few weeks getting settled into her new home. It didn't take Susan long to get comfortable in the small cabin. Jacob had bought her a few yards of material to make curtains for the windows and some for aprons. Jacob was a hard worker, but he always found time to spend with Susan in an effort to make her feel like it was her home. He was nice to her, as well as patient. He knew that living here was so much different from her former life, and it would take her sometime to adjust. She was finding him to be a good man who was good to her.

As time passed they gradually grew closer, but they were still getting to know each other. Jacob didn't expect her to fall in love with him instantly. It would take time for them to get used to each other.

# CHAPTER THREE

One morning in the fall, Jacob hitched up the wagon. He was going out into the forest to cut wood for cooking and for the fireplace to warm the cabin during the winter that would soon be coming. They would stack it near the cabin so it was easier to get at if the weather was bad.

Susan packed Jacob a lunch, gave him a kiss then saw him off. She watched him as he drove the team of horses into the forest.

As soon as he disappeared, she returned to the cabin and began making a stew for dinner. She was sure he would be very hungry after cutting and stacking wood all day. She couldn't help but think about how well they were getting along as she made the stew. It crossed her mind that she might be falling in love with him, she knew that she had grown very fond of him.

Jacob took the wagon out to a place in the woods where he could cut the wood they would need for the winter. In order to make it easier, he took off his holster and gun and hung it on the side of the wagon so that they would not get in the way when he swung his ax. He leaned his rifle against the wagon wheel then unhitched the horses and hobbled them so they could graze while he worked.

Jacob had been working for several hours when he heard something behind him. He turned to look and saw four men sitting on horses looking at him. One of the men had his rifle pointed at him. He immediately recognized one of the men. It was Wilbur Smith, his nearest neighbor, and not a very friendly man.

Wilbur Smith was a big man with a barrel chest, broad shoulders, and a pot belly. He was the richest man in the area; and if you bothered to ask anyone in the area who had the nerve to speak ill of Smith, they would say he was also the meanest man around. He was a man who was used to getting his way.

"What are you doing on my property?" Jacob asked sharply. "You're trespassing. Get the hell out of here."

"This is the last time I'm going to ask you. Sell me your ranch and get out, or else," Smith demanded.

"I will not sell it to you, ever," Jacob said as he moved closer to the wagon.

"Not another step closer to the wagon," Smith said sharply. "And drop the ax."

Jacob stopped, looked at the man holding the gun on him then dropped the ax. As soon as he dropped the ax, the big man turned and nodded to his men. Two of the men immediately got off their horses and walked toward Jacob while a third man held the reins of their horses.

Jacob knew what was about to happen. He slowly backed away, but they continued to get closer to him. He was wishing he had not moved so far away from his weapons, and that he had heard them sooner.

When they were close enough, Jacob lunged at them, knocking both of the men down. He began beating on one of the men in the hope of getting him out of the fight quickly and hopefully get a chance to grab his pistol.

Just as Jacob grabbed the gun, the other man got to his feet and came up behind Jacob. He struck Jacob alongside his head with his fist, causing Jacob to drop the gun and roll away from the man he had been beating. The man who had struck Jacob from behind began kicking and hitting Jacob. Each blow made it harder for Jacob to defend himself. The beating soon made it impossible for Jacob to get up and fight back.

The man that had been knocked down soon joined in beating Jacob. They beat Jacob mercilessly until he could no longer fight at all. The final blow came when one of them struck Jacob in the head with the butt of his rifle while Jacob was down and unable to defend himself.

"That's enough," Smith finally said.

"He's going to die if he ain't cared for," the young cowboy who was holding the reins of the two horses said.

"So what. It'll save us a lot of trouble if he does."

"His wife will know who done it," the cowboy said with a hint of fear in his voice as he looked at Smith.

"No one will believe her. Even if they do, it will be her word against mine; and no one around here would dare say a word against me," Smith said giving the young cowboy a nasty look.

"You two, get on your horses and let's get out of here."

"What about them horses? You just goin' to leave 'um here?" Smith's foreman, Jesse Jones, asked.

"No. We'll take the horses, but leave the wagon. Maybe they will think the Indians killed him and took his horses," Smith said with a grin and a slight chuckle.

As soon as the hobbles had been taken off the horses, they rode off taking the horses with them. The young cowboy looked back over his shoulder as they rode away leaving Jacob on the ground, bleeding and only half conscious. He was feeling a little sick to his stomach at what they had done. He was sure it would get out that he was there when Jacob was beaten. He wanted no part of it. When he got back to the ranch, he packed his belongings and rode away, heading west into the Wyoming Territory.

The day passed slowly for Susan even though she kept busy washing clothes, cooking a meal, and sewing a dress. As it grew late, Susan began to worry about Jacob. She stood in the doorway looking in the direction that Jacob had taken in the hope of seeing him soon. The later it got, the more concerned she became about him.

When Jacob failed to return by dinnertime, Susan couldn't wait any longer. She went to the barn and saddled their only remaining horse and went looking for him. After more than an hour of searching for him, she found him lying on the ground in the forest a short distance from the wagon.

Susan got off the horse and ran to him then knelt down beside him. She carefully lifted his head up and put it in her lap as she tried to comfort him. She took hold of the edge of her apron and began wiping the blood from his face. There was no doubt that he had been beaten, but he was still alive. She wasn't sure what to do for him. She needed to take him back to the cabin to tend to his wounds, but the horses used to pull the wagon were nowhere in sight.

"Oh, Jacob, what happened to you?" she cried hoping he could hear her.

Jacob slowly opened his eyes and looked up at her. His breathing was slow and shallow, and there was blood coming from his nose, mouth and ears.

"I'm sorry," he said softly, then coughed once before taking his last breath and fell limp in her arms.

Susan held him for a long time as tears filled her eyes as she cried for him. After crying for a while, she began to understand the reality of her situation. She was now alone, and she would have to do what had to be done by herself.

Looking down at Jacob, she began to realize she could not leave Jacob lying there, nor could she sit there holding him. As she looked at him, Susan remembered the promise Jacob had made to her before they were married. He had fulfilled his promise to do everything he could to make her happy right up until he was murdered. It was now time to do what she had to do for him. After only three months of marriage, Jacob was dead and she needed to bury him.

Susan brought her horse close to the wagon and tied it there. She struggled to get Jacob's body close to the horse and then up over the saddle. Once she had him on the horse, she led the horse back to the cabin. It was dark by the time she got back. The only light was from a half moon in the clear sky.

She tied the horse in front of the cabin while she got a lantern and a shovel from the barn. She lit the lantern then took her husband out to a small hill behind the cabin at the edge of the forest where she dug a grave and buried him. After saying a short prayer she had learned while at the orphanage, she returned to the cabin where she laid down on their bed and cried herself to sleep.

When Susan woke the next morning, she looked around the small cabin. For the first time since she had come to the valley with Jacob, she was alone, and she began to cry again. It wasn't long before she began to realize crying would not change anything. She would have to pull herself together and make some decisions.

Her first thought was that she was all alone to fend for herself. Her second thought was she really didn't have any place to go. To return to Chicago would only put her back in the same situation she had escaped from by marrying Jacob. Even if she wanted to leave the valley ranch, which was now rightfully hers, she only had one horse to leave on since her other two horses had been taken by whoever had killed her husband.

For her to travel on one horse she would certainly be limited to what she would be able to take with her. Although she had a wagon out in the woods, one horse would not be able to pull the wagon over the winding trail out of the valley even if she took only a few of her belongings with her. She thought about taking the horse and riding out of the valley to report to the sheriff what happened to Jacob.

Suddenly her thoughts turned to what Jacob had told her the evening before he went out into the woods. He had told her that a man by the name of Wilbur Smith was very angry at him because Jacob had filed a land claim for the valley first. Rumor had it Smith was a mean man who was used to getting anything he wanted and would do anything to get it. Smith wanted the small valley where Jacob had built his cabin to share with Susan.

Susan sat in front of the fireplace in the small cabin. Her eyes were puffy from crying. As she stared into the fire, watching the flames flicker, she thought about her situation. She wondered if Mr. Smith had killed, or had her husband killed, believing she would leave so he could get the valley for himself. It disturbed her to think a man would kill her husband for no other reason than to get the small valley ranch for himself, especially since he already owned most of the land south and west of the valley. It quickly came to her that there were people who had killed for a lot less.

It occurred to her that if she left the valley ranch, Smith might come into the valley and burn the cabin down leaving her with no shelter for the winter, forcing her to leave. That seemed a likely possibility, one she could not overlook.

Suddenly her thoughts were disturbed by the sound of horses out in front of the cabin. She stood up and went to the window, then slowly drew back the curtain just enough to be able to look out to see who was out there.

She saw three men on horses in front of her cabin looking around as if looking to see if there was anyone there. Each of them was well armed, but didn't have guns in their hands. Two of the men looked like cowboys. They wore cowboy hats, work shirts, chaps and had saddles with ropes rolled and tied to the saddle as well as bedrolls.

However, one of the men looked more like a businessman. He was wearing a brown suit with a vest. He had a cowboy hat that looked almost new, no sweat stains on the hat band and it was in good condition. He also had a gold watch chain across his more than ample belly. The look on his face was that of a man who was all business. His eyes were cold and hard looking. He had the look of a man who hated the whole world.

To Susan, he just looked mean. That thought made her wonder if the big man was Wilbur Smith. From the description her husband had given her, she quickly realized it was Wilbur Smith.

She wasn't sure what she should do. It came to her that she was not going to let him take away from her the only place she had ever been able to call her own. It was her home and she would not let him have it. Jacob would expect nothing less of her, she thought.

"He is not going to get my ranch if I can help it," she said to herself as she stepped away from the window, straightened up and pulled her shoulders back, then took a deep breath.

"Mrs. McDonald," Smith said in a loud, deep, booming voice. "I am Wilbur Smith. I want to talk to you, NOW!"

The sound of his voice did not make his words sound at all like a request, but rather a demand, even threatening. His voice frightened her, but she knew she couldn't let him know how frightened she really was of him. She picked up the double-barreled shotgun her husband had always kept next to the door and looked at it as if it was something she was certain she would need. She pulled back the hammer on each barrel. She then reached out to open the door, but before opening the door she took another deep breath in the hope of settling her fears. As soon as she felt she was ready, she jerked open the door, quickly stepped just outside the door and pointed the shotgun directly at Smith.

"Mr. Smith," she said in as firm a voice as she could. "I do not take kindly to you, or anyone else, coming on my property and yelling at me."

He looked at the small young woman as she stood in doorway. He could see she was nervous even if she was putting up a good front, and she did manage to hold the shotgun very steady. He didn't like the fact that it was pointed right at him.

"I've come here - - -," he said, but was quickly interrupted before he could finish.

"I don't care why you are here. You are trespassing on my land. I suggest you and your men get off my land before I shoot you right where you are," she said putting up the best show of strength she could muster.

She raised the shotgun to her shoulder while keeping it pointed directly at Smith's chest. He looked at it for only a second or two before he glared at her, then angrily swung his horse around and rode off at a gallop with his two ranch hands following along behind him.

Susan stood at the door of the cabin with the shotgun still pointed at them, and watched the three men ride away. It wasn't until they disappeared into the narrow canyon that came into the valley, and well out of range of her shotgun, that she lowered the shotgun and let out a sigh of relief. She was proud of herself for standing up to him, but it only took a second or two for her to realize it would not be the last time she would hear from him.

From what her husband had told her about him, and after seeing him, it was enough to make her believe it was definitely not over. The expression of anger on his face before he turned his horse and rode away confirmed her belief that she would have to deal with him again, and probably soon.

As soon as they were out of sight, she went back inside the cabin, shut the door and locked it, then collapsed on a

chair still gripping the shotgun. It took several minutes
before she could get herself breathing normally again. Once
she regained her composure, she set the shotgun on the floor
beside the chair.

"How am I going to be able to keep my valley ranch
from a man like that," she said as she looked around the
cabin.

Susan had to come up with a plan; a plan that she hoped
would discourage him from bothering her. The more she
thought about Mr. Smith, the more she began to realize she
would probably have to kill him, or he would kill her. She
would have to be watchful at all times. Everything she did
and everywhere she went, she would carry a gun. She would
put one of Jacob's rifles in the barn in case he or his men
came around while she was caring for her only horse and the
few chickens she had in and around the barn. She would
keep a shotgun along with a second rifle next to the door in
the cabin, and when she slept, she would sleep with a pistol
under her pillow. She would also wear one of Jacob's pistols
on her hip at all times when she was outside the cabin.

Susan got up from her chair and took a rifle out to the
barn, putting it close to one of the windows. When she had
done that, she went back to the cabin and made sure all the
weapons she had were loaded, easy to get at and ready to
use. When she thought she was as ready as she could be, she
made a vow that she would defend her valley ranch or die
trying.

# CHAPTER FOUR

For the next week or so, things were pretty quiet in the valley. Nothing much happened, but Susan still had the feeling that she was being watched. She didn't see anyone hanging around. She carried a gun everywhere she went, but she didn't wander off very far from the cabin or the barn. She was afraid if she got too far from them, Smith's men would see it as an opportunity to burn down the cabin and barn.

Every time she went outside to go to the barn to care for her horse or to pick a few vegetables from the small garden next to the cabin, a strange feeling would come over her. The feeling was one that seemed to warn her of danger, or that someone was spying on her from the edge of the forest. It caused her to become more vigilant, even to the point of putting her hand on the gun at her hip as she walked to the barn or to her garden.

On a bright sunny day while she was picking carrots from her small garden close to the cabin, she saw a man come riding up out of the narrow canyon leading into the valley. She ran into the cabin and quickly grabbed her shotgun. She stood inside the cabin by the window and watched and waited for the man to come close enough for her shotgun to be effective, if she thought she had to use it.

As the rider got closer to the cabin and within range of the shotgun, she stepped out in the doorway of the cabin and pointed the shotgun at him. The rider held his hands out away from his gun as he slowly rode closer to the cabin.

"That's close enough," she said, her voice firm and steady.

The rider stopped only a few yards from her, then looked down at her from the saddle. He said nothing, but simply leaned down and reached out his hand toward her. In his hand was a letter. Susan was hesitant to move any closer to him, and didn't dare take her eyes off him.

"Just drop the letter and leave," she said as she held the shotgun in both hands making sure it was pointed directly at him.

The man looked at her for a minute, then grinned. He dropped the letter on the ground, swung his horse around and rode off at a gallop. Susan stood watching him as he rode back to the narrow canyon. She waited until she was sure the man had left the valley before she walked over, bent down and picked up the letter. She glanced toward where the man had gone then looked at the letter. She slowly opened it and read it. The letter simply read, "GET OUT".

Once again she looked toward where the man had gone, then slowly backed into the cabin while glancing around to see if there might be someone else hiding in the woods. She saw no one.

As soon as she was inside the cabin, she quickly closed and bolted the door then set the shotgun down next to it. She looked at the letter again. Even though the letter was not signed, there was no doubt in her mind who the letter was from and what it meant.

Susan knew if she didn't leave the valley, Smith would put in motion a strong effort to force her to leave. She was also sure he would not hesitate to kill her, if he had to, in order to take her small valley ranch from her. In this deserted place, there would be no one to stop him, and no one would ever know what happened to her. Susan took the letter and sat down at the table.

Feeling the weight of the hopelessness of her situation, she put her hands over her face as she started to cry. After a short cry, she wiped the tears from her face and looked around the room.  She had to admit it wasn't really much of a cabin, and when she thought about it, she began to realize it wasn't much of a ranch, either.  She only had a few dozen cows and two young bulls, five chickens and a horse.  Even though it was not much of a ranch, it was all she had. Everything she had in the world was right there.  That thought made her feel very lonely.

With that thought in mind, she folded her hands in front of her and made a vow.  She would die right here before she would give in to Mr. Smith.  She would never sell the ranch to him, and she would fight to her last breath in an effort to keep her ranch.

She then bowed her head and said a little prayer asking for someone to help her.  If there was no one who could help her, she would spend her last days on earth in the little valley fighting to keep her ranch out of Smith's hands.

Time passed slowly as Susan struggled to keep the small ranch going.  Mr. Smith made it difficult for her.  During the next month or so, she noticed her cattle were disappearing. She had not seen who had taken them because they had been taken at night, a few at a time.  She was pretty sure Mr. Smith had given the order to his men to steal the cattle. There was nothing she could do about it.  She could not watch over her cattle twenty-four hours a day.  She had to sleep sometime.

Late one afternoon when the sun was low in the sky, she stepped out the door of the barn after feeding her horse.  The sun was reflecting off something bright at the edge of the woods.  She quickly backed into the barn and grabbed the rifle she had left in the barn in case she was trapped there. She looked out the window, but she didn't see anything for several minutes.

Suddenly, she saw the bright light again.  It took a minute or so for her to realize that the sun was reflecting off something just inside the wooded area across the creek, and whatever it was, it was moving just a bit. She concentrated on the spot where she had seen the light. After over a minute of watching the same spot in the woods, something moved. It was a horse. It was at that moment Susan realized the sun was reflecting off the bit of a horse's bridle just inside the woods.

Susan quickly placed her rifle on the window ledge then looked out the window toward where she had seen the reflection. It took her a minute or so before she could make out Mr. Smith sitting on his horse watching her from the woods. He was at the edge of the woods and probably planning something, but more importantly he was on her property. He was trespassing.

She stepped back a little from the window, put the rifle to her shoulder then laid the end of the barrel on the windowsill to steady it. She took careful aim at Smith, then slowly pulled the trigger, just as Jacob had taught her. There was a load bang and the rifle recoiled into her shoulder. When she looked out the window again, she saw Mr. Smith riding off as fast as his horse could carry him, and he was holding his arm. She was sure she had hit him, but apparently not hard enough to knock him out of the saddle.

Susan smiled to herself as she watched him ride away, but the smile quickly faded from her face when she thought about what she had done. If she had killed him, it might have been the end of it. But the fact that she had just wounded him was likely to make it just the beginning. The fact she had taken a shot at him would make him mad and more determined than ever to take the valley ranch away from her. She would have to be very careful and never let her guard down, not even for a second.

Over the next few days, Susan didn't see Mr. Smith, but saw one or two of his ranch hands on her property. They just seemed to be watching her from a distance. She made it a point of not shooting at them, although she had the right to protect her land. She would bide her time and wait until they either made a full scale attack in an effort to take her small valley ranch by force, or they moved in close enough for her to get a really good shot at one of them, a shot that would kill or completely disable the trespasser. Whatever they tried, she knew she would put up a fight they would not soon forget.

As much as she didn't like the idea of killing someone, she knew it was the only thing they would understand. It was them or her. They had given her no choice.

Susan wondered how long she would be able to hold onto the ranch before Mr. Smith would kill her. With winter coming on she didn't dare leave the valley to get help for fear he would burn down the cabin and barn so she would have no place to live. She would have to leave for at least a couple of days, making it easy for Smith to take control of the land.

In his effort to force Susan off the land and out of the valley, Smith had his men run off the remaining cattle, including the calves that had been born last spring. The vegetables she had planted in the spring were now large enough to be edible. Each morning she would go out and pick some to store for the winter which was fast approaching.

# CHAPTER FIVE

Sitting at a table in a Saloon on the main street of Cheyenne was a man by the name of Frank Griswold. He was a tall man in his early thirties with dark brown hair that came down over his collar, a dark handlebar mustache and deep dark brown eyes that didn't miss anything. He carried a .45 caliber Colt Peacemaker on his right hip and a .38 caliber Smith and Wesson in his belt. He wore a buckskin shirt and black flock pants with the legs stuffed in the tops of his tall black boots. He had a small knife sticking out of the top of his right boot and a fairly large knife on his belt. He looked like a man who was sure of himself and his ability. He also looked like a man who could take care of himself.

Frank was a man of many talents, not the least of which was his ability to handle a gun, both rifles and pistols, and a knife if need be. He had been a town marshal for several months in Silver City, but didn't like the confinement to the small town it imposed on him. He quit the town marshal's job and turned to being a gun for hire, but not by just anyone. He occasionally hired out to stagecoach companies, fright companies and the railroad companies to help protect gold shipments from the mines or banks and other locations. He also hired out to cattle ranchers who were in need of a fast gun to protect their cattle from rustlers. He had even done a little bounty hunting when he needed a little money and had nothing else to do. He had a strong sense of helping those who needed help, and a strong sense of what was right and wrong.

Frank had ended up in Cheyenne after completing a job for the Cheyenne to Deadwood Stagecoach Company. His job had been to protect a shipment of gold from Deadwood to a bank in Cheyenne where it was to be shipped back east by railroad.

After completing his job without incident, he collected his fee then decided to take a little time off to relax and have a drink. His plans were to pack up his meager belongings in the morning and catch the stagecoach back to Custer City where he had left his horse to rest due to a slightly strained ligament. After getting his horse, he would continue to Deadwood to see what job he might be able to pick up there.

While he sat at the table in the saloon drinking a beer, a young man came in. He had the appearance of a cowboy. The gun on his hip was nothing special. It looked like the kind of gun most cowboys wore as part of the job, a .45 caliber Colt. The young man was short with blond hair and blue eyes. He was wearing a cowboy hat, a plaid shirt, chaps over well-worn jeans, and boots that had seen better days. His clothes were covered with dust indicating he might have just arrived in town after traveling some distance.

The cowboy stopped and stood just inside the door of the saloon as he looked around. Frank couldn't decide if the young cowboy was looking for someone, or if he couldn't make up his mind if he wanted to come into the saloon for a drink. Frank decided to ask the young cowboy.

"Say, young fellow, you looking for someone, or looking to have a drink?"

The young cowboy turned and looked at the man sitting at the table. He wasn't sure, but he thought he had seen him before. If the man was who he thought he was, he knew him to be someone who worked within the law, at least as far as he knew. He walked over to the table and put his hands on the back of a chair and leaned forward.

"Sit down, if you've a mind to. You look like you could use a beer," Frank said as he pointed at the empty chair.

"Thanks," the young cowboy said.

The cowboy pulled out a chair and sat down while Frank waved to the barkeep to bring the kid a beer.

"Do I know you?" the cowboy asked.

"You might. The name's Frank Griswold," he said as he watched the barkeep place a beer in front of the young cowboy.

"What's your name?" Frank asked.

"Billy Roth. I thought I recognized you," Billy said. "You work for the stagecoach line."

"I'm done with that job. I'm not working for anyone right now. You got something on your mind?"

"In a way. I'm looking for the sheriff. Do you happen to know where I can find him?"

"I heard the sheriff's out of town and will be gone for several days. He went to Rapid City for something. I think he went to pick up a prisoner."

"Oh," he said sounding very disappointed.

"You in some sort of trouble?"

"No. No, not me," he said almost too quickly and with a hint of nervousness in his voice.

"Why don't you tell me about it? Maybe I can help."

Billy looked down at his hands on the table for a moment before looking up again.

"I ain't sure."

"If you got something to say, just say it. I'll decide if I can help."

"Well, I ain't sure, but I think there's a young woman over near Hell's Canyon, and she's all alone."

"How is it you know she's alone?"

"A guy I met while working in Wyoming told me about her, that's all," he said rather sharply.

"I've heard of only one young woman living in the area you're talking about and that would be Mrs. McDonald. Mrs. McDonald has a husband. Did you see her husband?"

"No! Well, that's what he said."

Again the cowboy was rather sharp and quick in his response. Billy seemed very nervous which gave Frank the feeling he was hiding something, or he knew more than he was saying. He looked at the cowboy for a minute before he spoke.

"What were you doing over that way?"

"I – ah – I mean he was just passin' through."

"I find that hard to believe. I hear the McDonald's ranch is way off the beaten path. In fact, I hear it's hard to find if you don't know where it is and how to get there."

"You been there?"

"No, but I know the country around there. There has to be a couple of dozen little valleys in that area, some haven't had anyone in them except Indians, and some of them haven't seen a human footprint in a very long time, if at all."

"He said he didn't see no husband. She was alone. That's all I gotta say. You goin' ta check it out?"

"If he didn't see her husband, then there might be something wrong. Since I have nothing better to do at the moment, and it's on my way back to Deadwood, I'll stop in Custer City and pick up my horse then go out that way and see if I can find the place. If I find it, I'll have a talk with Mrs. McDonald."

Frank watched as the young cowboy stood up, turned and walked out the door without saying another word. He even left the beer Frank had bought for him untouched. Frank stared at the door after the cowboy left wondering what it was the cowboy was not telling him. Frank reached over and picked up the beer and took a sip. As he sipped on the beer he began to think about what the cowboy had told him.

It was rather late in the day, to catch the stagecoach to Custer City where he planned to get his horse at the livery stable. Once he had his horse, he could head out to check on

Mrs. McDonald.  Frank decided he would get his gear together and leave on the morning stagecoach.

Frank took the morning stagecoach to Custer City. When he arrived in Custer City, he went to the livery stable and paid the owner for caring for his horse.  He then went to the Land Office to find out where the McDonald ranch was located.  He thought it could take him several days, maybe as much as a week, just to find the place.  Once he had the information he needed, he returned to his room in the hotel to pack up what he would need, which was everything he owned plus some food, then get a good night's sleep.

When the morning sun was coming up over the horizon, it found Frank Griswold ready to leave the small town of Custer City and head west toward Hell's Canyon deep in the Southern Black Hills.  As he rode, he wondered if Mrs. McDonald was really living alone.  If she was, the question that came to mind was what had happened to her husband? Had he been killed by someone, or had he died as a result of an accident, or maybe he died of some sickness?

The thought passed through Frank's mind that it might be a waste of his time to look for her.  It was possible the young cowboy simply didn't see Mr. McDonald.  Since Frank was without work at the moment, he thought he could take the time to check it out and make sure everything was all right.

On his way toward Hell's Canyon, Frank made a brief stop at Four Mile Stage Stop to inquire about the McDonalds.  He talked to the woman running the stage stop.

"Howdy," Frank said as he rode up to the hitching rail.

"Howdy.  You're Frank Griswold, aren't you?" Mary Miller asked.

"Yeah," Frank said as he stepped down from the saddle.

"What brings you out this way?  I thought I saw you on the stage going east just yesterday."

"You did. Do you know Jacob McDonald?"

"Yeah, sure. I ain't seen him for, ah, couple of months or so. He's got himself a wife, ya know."

"I've heard," Frank said.

"I've only seen them twice. Once when he brought his new wife out here, and once when they came in to get some supplies, a couple of months ago."

"Have you heard if anything has happened to Jacob?"

"No, can't say I have. Is there something wrong?" Mary said with a concerned look on her face.

"Not that I know of, but there could be."

"The last time I saw Jacob, he looked pretty healthy. Why? What's your interest in Jacob?" Mary asked knowing that Frank did a little bounty hunting from time to time.

"I heard Mrs. McDonald was all alone at that ranch they have back in the hills."

"I never heard nothing like that. Like I said, they were here together the last time I saw them. They both looked happy and healthy."

"Well, I think I'll see if I can find their place just to make sure everything is okay."

"That sounds like a good idea. Mrs. McDonald's a city woman, ya know. She might have a hard time livin' alone out there," Mary said with a concerned look on her face.

"That's what I was thinking," Frank said.

Frank went into the stage stop and bought a few things he thought he might need. He then said goodbye to the stage stop manager. Frank untied his horse and swung up in the saddle. He turned his horse and headed deep into the Black Hills.

Frank was three days out of Custer City before he found a narrow trail he thought might get him close to the small valley where the McDonald's ranch was located. He turned his horse and began following it.

As he rode along the narrow trail, he noticed the sky was clouding up. It wouldn't be long before he would need to find a place to make a shelter and hunker down for the night. It was fairly cold and the sky looked like it might snow if it got much colder.

Just as Frank came over the small ridge and started toward a grove of trees where he thought he could build a shelter and settle in for the night, he felt a sharp pain in his side followed by the loud crack of a rifle shot. He dove off his horse and tried to move to cover behind a nearby tree. When he was only a couple of feet from the protection of the tree, he felt the pain of another bullet as it ripped through his leg. Frank fell to the ground and laid still. Moving as little as possible, he slipped his spare gun out of his belt then waited quietly and listened for any sounds of movement. Being in no condition to fight back, he laid on the ground without moving. If there was more than one person out there, it would be difficult to make a fight of it, but he was not about to give up without a fight if whoever had attacked him decided to press the attack. He hoped whoever it was would think he had killed him and simply ride off.

Frank stayed very still and listened for any sound that might tell him if someone was coming closer. He didn't hear anything for what seemed like a long time. After waiting for several minutes, he heard the sound of a horse running away. He took a deep breath and relaxed for a moment or two.

Relieved that his attacker had left, probably thinking he had finished off the intruder, Frank slipped his gun back into his belt then dragged himself up to a nearby tree and leaned against it. Removing his bandana from around his neck, he wrapped it around the wound to his leg in the hope of stopping the bleeding. He opened his coat and pulled his shirt loose from his waist. He took his knife and cut part of the shirttail off and used it to cover the wound in his side. He was in a great deal of pain, but he knew he needed help, and he needed it soon. He was afraid that if he tried to stay there, he might bleed to death before anyone would find him.

His horse was standing only a short distance from him. Frank called to the horse and the large animal came to him. He reached up and grabbed a stirrup then pulled himself up to a standing position. The wound in his side burned and made him feel lightheaded. He took a few deep breaths to clear his head then reached out and took hold of the saddle horn. He tried to pull himself up so he could get a foot in the stirrup, but failed. He waited for a moment or two to let the pain subside, then tried again to pull himself up and into the saddle. It took two more tries before he was able to get in the saddle, each try making the pain almost unbearable.

Once in the saddle, he nudged the horse in its sides with his spurs and the horse began to walk away from the tree. After going a short distance, Frank guided the horse into a narrow canyon just off the trail where he hoped to be safe from another attack. It had just started to rain when he found the entrance to a narrow canyon. He hoped he might find help at the end of the canyon.

The rain was a steady, cold rain that was slowly drenching him. With the heavy rain, he was pretty sure he would not be followed because it would wash away any tracks his horse would make in the soft, wet ground.

The effort it had taken him to get back in the saddle had drained him of much of his energy. He had to lean forward and place an arm on either side of the horse's neck in order to keep his balance and to help him stay in the saddle. He knew if he fell from the saddle, he would not be able to get back in it again. He was also sure he would not live long if he fell from the saddle.

The large horse walked slowly up the narrow canyon, stepping around the boulders and over the narrow ditches that were almost full of water. The large dapple gray horse continued to travel all night, plodding slowly along the narrow trail that wandered through the canyon. The horse splashed through the puddles and mud as it continued to move deeper into the mountains. It was almost as if the horse knew where it was going. It seemed to know it had to be very careful to keep the man slumped over its neck in the saddle.

During the night, the horse had managed to move along at a slow but steady pace. It continued to rain for most of the night and for a good part of the early morning before it slowed to a steady, gentle drizzle about mid-morning. The horse had covered a lot of ground while still keeping its rider on its back.

Suddenly, the horse came out of the narrow canyon into an open field. It stopped and looked around as if it didn't know where to go from there. The field spread out into a small mountain valley with rich, thick, green grass. The valley was surrounded by heavily forested hills backed by rocky ridges jutting up toward the sky and disappearing into the low hanging clouds. It appeared there was only one way in or out of the valley, and that was through the canyon the horse had just come through.

The horse stood for a moment or two as if it was trying to decide if it should continue. Its head and ears came up when it saw through the mist a log cabin near the edge of the forest partway up the valley. The animal could also see a barn and a corral, but there were no horses in the corral. A barn meant food and shelter to the horse.

The horse slowly began to move toward the barn. It had made it almost to the corral when the man on its back slipped to one side and slid out of the saddle, falling to the wet ground with a thud. The horse stopped and stood next to the man as if to protect him. The horse lowered its head close to the man's face as if to see if he was still alive, then raised its head, looked toward the cabin and whinnied. It whinnied several times before there was any kind of a response from the cabin.

# CHAPTER SIX

Susan was sitting on a stool in front of the fireplace. She had hung a cast-iron pot on the fireplace hook and swung it over the fire. The pot was filled with small pieces of beef, chunks of carrots and potatoes, and slices of onions. She wanted it to simmer slowly so it would be ready to eat later in the day.

It was a good day to have a fire in the cabin. The fall weather was cold and damp, and it had been raining all night and most of the morning. It was now just a steady drizzle as a mist sort of filled the air under the clouds that hung low over the valley. If the temperature continued to drop, it could start snowing soon, Susan thought as she stirred the stew.

As Susan looked into the fire, she thought of her husband and tears came into her eyes again. She was not sure if it was because his death had left her all alone, or if it was because she had no one to help her protect her valley ranch. Maybe it was because she knew that without any help, she would lose the valley ranch to Smith, and maybe her life. And maybe it was the fact she and Jacob had not had time enough to fall in love like she hoped would happen with time.

The one thing she knew was Jacob had kept his promise to her, and he had been good to her. Maybe the tears were because she was beginning to love him, but just hadn't realized it, yet.

She cried for several minutes before she came to the realization that crying was not going to change her situation one bit. She needed to do whatever she could to keep the ranch. The ranch was all she had. She had no family to turn to for help, and she knew no one who could or would help her. She had even prayed for help. She also knew that if she left the valley to report what was going on to the sheriff, it was likely she would return to a cabin and barn that had been burned to the ground.

Susan's thoughts of her husband and her current situation were suddenly disturbed by the sound of a horse. She had no idea how long she had been crying, but she quickly wiped her eyes, got up and moved to the door. She picked up the shotgun she kept next to the door, then moved to the nearby window and drew back the curtain just enough to see outside. All she could see was a horse with a saddle and bridle on it, but no rider, standing in the wet grass looking toward the cabin. The horse looked like it had been out in the rain for a very long time and that it may have traveled a long way.

She went to the door and slowly opened it. Susan looked out at the horse standing in the light rain. At first she didn't see the man lying on the ground next to the horse. As she stood in the doorway with the double-barreled shotgun firmly held in her hands, she wondered where the rider was and where the horse had come from. She wondered if it might be a trap to get her to come out of the cabin. She carefully looked around, but didn't see anyone who might be lurking about. She knew full well that to leave the cabin without being very careful could mean her death.

Holding the shotgun tightly in her small hands, she slowly stepped out of the cabin onto the wet grass. She stopped and looked toward the corners of the cabin, then out toward the barn. When she didn't see anyone, she turned and looked at the horse again. It was at that moment she finally saw a man lying on the wet ground next to the horse.

The sight of the man on the ground surprised her. Being very cautious, she moved slowly toward the man. She kept her eyes moving and her shotgun pointed at the man just in case it was a trick.

When she got up close to him, she could see his face. The man's dark wavy hair was wet and matted against his pale face. He had a thick handlebar mustache and several days' growth of beard. His clothes were soaking wet and there was a bandana covered in blood wrapped around his right leg, and he wasn't moving. He looked like he might be dead. After taking a second to look around to see if there was anyone else nearby, she knelt down beside him and reached out to touch him to see if he was still alive.

Suddenly, his eyes flew open and his hand shot out grabbing her by the wrist. He had grabbed her so quickly that she dropped her shotgun. She didn't have a chance to get away from him.

As she tried to pull away from him, he pulled her over him. Her face was only inches from his. His eyes were dark and looked at her with hate in them.

He looked into her eyes and could see that she was terrified. As he slowly released his grip on her, his eyes closed and his hand fell limp at his side. He had passed out.

Susan sat back on her heels and looked at him while she took a moment to catch her breath. He had scared her. As soon as she had regained her composure, she reached out to him again, but she touched only his hand. He didn't move, but she could tell he was still alive. She could see his breath in the cold damp mid-morning air. There was little doubt in her mind he wouldn't live very long if she didn't get him off the cold, wet ground and into the warmth of her cabin.

She stood up and looked at the horse. The horse was standing there, not moving, just watching her. Susan moved toward the horse very slowly. The horse took a step back, but didn't really try to get away from her. She reached out and took hold of the reins while talking softly to the horse.

Once she had control of the horse, she moved alongside the it and took the rope off the saddle. She made a loop in the rope, then slipped it around the man and under his arms. Susan then tied the rope to the saddle horn.

After picking up her shotgun, she took hold of the reins of the horse and slowly led it toward the cabin. As the horse pulled his owner toward the cabin, Susan would glance back to make sure she was not causing any more injuries to the man. The horse pulled the man up close to the cabin then stopped.

As soon as she reached the cabin, Susan tied the horse to the hitching rail in front of the cabin. She took her shotgun inside and leaned it against the door, then returned to the man. She took the rope off him, then bent down and literally dragged him into the cabin, then shut the door.

Once she had him in the cabin, she took off his heavy sheepskin coat. She discovered he had also been shot in his right side. Susan removed his gun belt and hung it over the back of a chair. When she stripped him of his shirt, she could see a piece of his shirt had been placed over the wound in his side. From the look of the blood soaked piece of cloth, he had been bleeding for sometime. She decided she should bath him before she tended to his wounds to make sure he didn't have any other injuries. Once she had all his clothes off, she bathed him then put him on her bed.

When she had him lying on the bed, she put a towel under him to keep his blood off the bed. She removed the piece of cloth to check the wound in his right side. There was a bullet hole just below his ribs. There seemed to be a slight bit of drainage at the wound, but it didn't look like much. It had almost stopped bleeding.

Susan immediately got clean water and clean cloths then washed the wound. Once it was clean, she discovered there was still a bullet in the wound. She got a thin bladed knife and heated the blade so it would be clean. It took her several minutes to dig the bullet out of his side, but once it was out, she cleaned the wound again then put a clean piece of cloth over it. She then wrapped a long piece of cloth around his body to hold the dressing in place and tightly against the wound.

She turned her attention to the wound in the upper part of his right leg. She quickly examined the wound and found it not to be as serious as the one to his side. She also discovered the bullet had passed through his leg, but had apparently not hit anything vital such as a major blood vessel or the bone. It appeared as if the bleeding had stopped. She cleaned the wound and covered it with a piece of clean cloth, then wrapped a piece of cloth around his leg and secured it tightly to keep the dressing in place.

When she had done all she could for him, she covered him with a quilt in an effort to make him as comfortable as possible. She then added a couple of logs to the fire to warm the cabin.

Susan sat by the fire and watched him for a few minutes to make sure he was resting quietly. Satisfied that he was resting peacefully, she went to the window and looked out. The man's horse was standing in the rain with its head hanging down and looked like it could use a little help, too.

She turned and looked at the man again, then took her husband's pistol, put it in a holster and strapped it around her waist. After putting on a coat, Susan opened the door and looked around to make sure there was no one else around before she stepped outside. She untied the horse from the hitching rail and led it to the barn. She took the animal into the barn and put it in a stall. After taking the saddle off the horse, she put it over the top rail of a stall. She rubbed the horse down with a rag as best she could. When she was finished, she removed the bridle, then fed the horse, giving it a good helping of oats along with some hay.

With the horse settled in the stall, she took the man's bedroll, saddlebags and rifle from the saddle. She took a dry cloth and dried the man's saddle then took the man's bedroll, saddlebags and rifle into the cabin. She leaned his rifle next to the door, then put his bedroll and saddlebags on the floor next to his rifle.

Before taking her gun belt off, she took a minute to look outside again. She wanted to make sure no one had followed him. She didn't see anyone watching her or stalking around. It was easy to see no one would have been able to track the man into the valley ranch. The heavy rain that had ended only a short time before he showed up in front of her cabin would have washed away his tracks. It had also started to snow. With his horse in the barn, no one would know he was there.

She shut the door, turned around and looked at the man lying in her bed. The first thing she noticed was he had not moved since she put him there, but she could see his chest rise and fall with each breath. The thought passed through her mind that it had been a long time since a man had been in her bed. She was beginning to feel very much alone again, and very lonely.

Her husband had been killed a little over three months ago. She had been alone day after day ever since, with the exception of the visits Mr. Smith or his men had paid her in his effort to get her to leave her valley ranch. She was sure Mr. Smith was getting very impatient with her and no longer cared how he got his hands on her valley ranch.

Susan shook herself in an effort to get the feeling of loneliness off her mind. She took another look at the man in her bed. Now that he was cleaned up, she got her first really good look at him. She couldn't help but think he was a very nice looking man in a rugged sort of way. He looked strong and well built. His color had returned a bit now that he was warm and resting.

She wondered what kind of a man he was, and how he would treat a woman. She had to admonish herself for the thoughts running through her mind. There was a handsome, naked man lying under the quilt in her bed, and she was a young, healthy woman. The feelings she was having about him had to be because she was so lonely, and she had spent a long time alone with no one to talk to and no one to provide her with companionship. Susan had to look away from him in order to get her thoughts under control.

She sat down in her chair, cupped her face in her hands and began to cry. Living in the little mountain valley with no one to talk to and no one else around was not what she had expected when she married Jacob. She also came to the realization she hadn't really known Jacob all that well. He was a man who had lived alone for a long time. Jacob had been good to her, but it was a hard life being the only people in the valley, and a long way from any kind of store. The closest place was Four Mile Stage Stop, and that was at least fifteen miles away.

Even though Jacob and Susan had gotten along well, there was little love between them, something Susan had hoped would come with time. The truth was, there had not been enough time for them to really get to know each other all that well.

The day passed slowly for Susan. Every time she went to the fireplace to stir the stew she would look over at the man and wonder who he was and what he was doing in the valley. She wondered if he could be one of Mr. Smith's men. That thought began to worry her.

She glanced at the man's bedroll and saddlebags next to his rifle near the door where she had left them. She got up from the chair and walked over to the fireplace. She took a moment to stir the stew, then again looked at the man who was lying in her bed. He was still resting well.

Susan turned and looked at the saddlebags again, not sure if she should look inside them. Deciding there might be something in the saddlebags that would give her at least a clue who the man was and what kind of man was in her bed. She picked up the saddle bags and put them on the table.

Susan hesitated for a moment, first looking at the saddlebags then looking at the man. She was about to go through his personal belongings. There had to be something in the saddlebags that would tell her something about him, she thought. Maybe he had a girlfriend somewhere who was worried about him, or maybe he had a family; but more importantly, was he someone she should be worried about.

Taking a deep breath, she opened one side of the saddlebags. Inside she found a small pouch containing coffee and a bag with some hardtack biscuits. There were two shirts rolled up and one pair of pants. There was also a box of .45 caliber cartridges that would fit his pistol and rifle, and a box of .38 caliber cartridges that would fit the smaller gun he carried in his belt. What she found did nothing to tell her if he would be a danger to her once he regained consciousness.

After putting everything back in the saddlebags, she turned the saddlebags around and opened the other side. She found some jerky, a small amount of gold coins amounting to about twenty dollars total, and a small leather pouch. She opened the pouch and discovered two wanted posters, a letter from a stagecoach company, and a bank draft.

The letter was a request for his services as a guard for a gold shipment from Deadwood to Cheyenne. The bank draft was drawn on a Cheyenne bank in the amount of three hundred dollars, and showed that he had completed the services requested in the letter. The letter gave her a small bit of relief because it showed her that he was probably an honest man if he was asked to protect a gold shipment. It also told her that his name was Frank Griswold.

Susan just stood there looking at the letter for a moment, then turned and looked at the man in her bed. Her first thought was he might be someone who could help her, but quickly realized he was in no condition to help anyone, not even himself, at the moment. It would probably be some time before he could even get up. She put everything back in the saddle bags, then closed up the saddlebags and set it back by the door next to his bedroll.

Susan noticed that it was starting to get dark outside. It worried her that something might happen before Mr. Griswold would be able to help her.

Susan realized she had not eaten her dinner. She got up and fixed herself a large bowl of stew, set it on the table, then sat back down and began eating. She sat on the side of the table that would allow her to watch Mr. Griswold as he slept.

As she ate, she had a lot of things going through her mind. One of them was who shot Mr. Griswold. If it was one of Mr. Smith's gunmen, they might know what his horse looked like. If the horse should be seen, there was a strong possibility the horse would be recognized. If it was, they might be able to figure out Mr. Griswold is in her cabin. She would have to keep the horse out of sight, at least for a few days.

She knew she would have to protect Mr. Griswold as best she could until he was able to get around on his own. Susan looked at his rifle next to the door, then at his pistol on the back of the chair and the one next to the bed. All of them had been wet and his pistols were muddy from when he fell off the horse. She decided it would be a good idea to clean them and make sure they where ready to use. If nothing else, it would give her more weapons she could use to defend herself and her valley ranch.

When Susan finished eating, she took his guns and put them on the table. She began to carefully clean them one at a time. She was glad that Jacob had taught her how to clean their guns, as well as how to use them. While she cleaned them, she began to wonder why he was there. What had brought him to her cabin? She knew his horse had brought him there, but what was he doing in the area in the first place? Had someone written to him and asked him to come to investigate Mr. Smith's activities? Did someone know she was alone? All her questions were good questions, but none of them were going to get answered until he was awake and able to talk to her.

There was nothing else she could do for him tonight. After she finished cleaning and reloading his guns, she set the rifle next to the door along with her shotgun and laid the pistols on the end of the table where they would be in easy reach. She then cleaned up her dishes. Susan pulled the curtains over the windows before she lit her lantern.

Susan spent a good part of the evening sitting in her chair knitting. She would look at Mr. Griswold from time to time to make sure he was resting well. Susan thought about what she could do for him, but had no idea what more she could do. She would just have to wait and hope that he recovered, and hopefully soon.

As it grew late, she put her knitting up and walked over to the bed. She lifted up the quilt and checked his wounds. The bandages were dry, which was a good indication the bleeding had stopped. She turned down the lantern and got a quilt for herself, then sat down in her chair and covered herself with it. It was not a very restful night for her. Having a stranger in her cabin without knowing anything about him, or very little about him, caused her a great deal of concern. Every sound and every movement that Mr. Griswold made caused her to wake up and check on him, making it hard for her to get any real rest.

# CHAPTER SEVEN

When morning came, Susan woke and felt a cold chill in the cabin. Reluctantly, she gave up the warmth she had in the chair for the cold of the cabin by laying her quilt to the side as she stood up. Looking at the fireplace, she realized the fire had burned down to just a few embers. She immediately put several pieces of wood in the fireplace and blow gently on the hot embers causing the fire to flare up again. It wouldn't take long before the warmth of the fire spread throughout the small cabin.

Once she had the fire going and the cabin began to warm up, she looked over at her bed. Mr. Griswold looked like he was still sleeping. She wondered if he had been awake at any time during the night. She had heard him move a couple of times, but she didn't think he actually woke up.

Susan went over to the window, pushed the curtain to one side so she could look out. The rain had turned to snow just before she had gone to sleep, and it looked like it had been snowing fairly hard through the night. The snow had built up to well over a foot and it was still coming down hard. Seeing all that snow caused Susan to let out a sigh of relief. With that much snow, there was little chance anyone would be hanging around, or that anyone could have followed Mr. Griswold to the cabin. There was also little chance that Mr. Smith would be bothering her today.

She leaned up against the wall next to the window and gazed at the snow as it continued to fall. It was snowing so hard she could barely make out the barn. With the slight breeze, the snow was drifting into long narrow rows across the open spaces in front of the cabin. Some looked to be as deep as two to two and a half feet in many places. She couldn't help but enjoy it because she knew it would soon be so deep not even the best of horses could move in it, and she would be able to relax for the first time in weeks, a feeling she had not had since before her husband had been murdered.

Even Mr. Smith and his men would be snowed in and unable to come into the valley. This much snow could close the canyon leading into the valley for as long as a week, depending on how fast it melted once it quit snowing.

Suddenly there was a sound from behind her. She quickly turned and looked toward the bed. Mr. Griswold had groaned when he moved. From the look on his face, Susan was sure he was in pain, but there was nothing she could do about it. Just the fact he had moved gave her hope that he would survive. Susan got a damp cloth then walked over to the bed. She sat down on the edge of the bed, reached out and placed the damp cloth on his forehead.

Frank turned his head and looked up at her. There was a moment of confusion on his face as if he didn't recognize her, but it was soon followed by a slight smile.

"Mrs. McDonald?" he asked.

"Yes. How are you feeling?"

"I've felt better, but at least I'm alive."

Susan smiled, then explained how she had found him and what she had done for him. She told him that his horse had brought him to her cabin.

"I vaguely remember seeing you. Do you know where I saw you?"

"It was after you fell from your horse in front of my barn. I found you lying in the grass. Your horse told me you were there."

Frank looked a little confused by her statement, and asked, "He told you I was there?"

"Yes. He stood next to you and whinnied until I came out and saw you lying in the grass."

"Where is he now, do you know?"

"He is in the barn where he is safe, dry and well fed," Susan said with a grin.

"He always did know where to find shelter and food, especially food."

"Be glad he does."

"Oh, I am. I truly am," Frank said.

"You should rest now. I'll fix you something to eat in a little while."

"Yes, Ma'ma," he said then slowly closed his eyes.

Susan got up from the edge of the bed and went over to the fire. She started making some broth for him. It suddenly occurred to her that she had not even asked him why he was there. She turned, looked at him and started to talk to him, but realized he was sleeping. She smiled to herself as she thought he had immediately done what she had told him to do, but quickly realized he probably slept because he was tired. His lose of blood probably had a lot to do with it, too.

While looking at him, she once again wondered what kind of a man he might be. The fact he had a letter from the railroad company and two wanted posters gave her the idea that he was not only a man hired by companies that needed someone who was honest, trustworthy and could use a gun; but he was probably a bounty hunter from time to time, as well. It was easy for her to understand that a man like him might be violent, even brutal, at times. The question that came to her mind was how he would treat her once he no longer needed her to care for him.

She suddenly wondered why that thought came to mind. Maybe it was because her only contact with another human since she lived there, other than her husband, was with Mr. Smith, and he wasn't the kind of person she wanted to see.

As the day wore on, Frank would wake up for a little while then doze off again. It was starting to get dark when Susan walked over to the bed and gently sat down on the edge of it. He opened his eyes as he turned his head and looked up at her.

"How are you feeling?" she asked.

"Better, I think. I don't hurt as much. My leg seems to ache more than being painful, but I'm sure it will change as soon as I get up and try to walk."

"I'm sure it will, but you're not getting up, not yet anyway. I don't want you opening up your wounds by getting up too soon. How would you like some broth? You should eat something."

"I would like that," he said.

Susan got up and walked over to the fireplace to get him a bowl of broth. As she ladled some broth into a bowl, she wondered why he was in her valley. She decided it was time to ask him.

Susan turned and carried the broth over to the small table next to the bed. She set it down then leaned over him to put another pillow under his head to prop him up a little. In her effort to help him sit up, she caused him to groan in pain.

"I'm sorry," she said looking down at him not wishing to cause him anymore pain.

"It's okay. It will be a little while before I'm able to move at all without it hurting."

She smiled at him then again helped him sit up. In helping him sit up she leaned over him again. His face was very close to her breasts as she reached above his head to position his pillow. She looked down at him and found him looking at her. It embarrassed her a little to see him watching her so closely, and being so physically close that she could feel his breath against her neck. She immediately sat back and straightened her dress before picking up the bowl of broth, then started feeding him.

Nothing was said between them until the broth was gone. He had made Susan a little nervous by watching her so closely, and being so close to her. When she started to get up, he reached out and took hold of her arm, only much gentler than he did when he had grabbed her out in front of the barn.

She stopped and looked at him, wondering what he wanted. When he just looked at her for a moment, she sat back down on the edge of the bed.

"Mrs. McDonald, I hope this will not upset you, but where is your husband?"

She turned her face away from him and looked at the floor for a moment, took a deep breath, then turned back to answer him.

"My husband is dead," she said softly, suddenly remembering that Mr. Griswold might be a bounty hunter. "Why? Were you looking for him?"

"No. I had heard you were married to Jacob McDonald, a good man. When I was told you were up here alone, I decided I would check and see if you were all right."

"Who told you I was alone?" she asked thinking the only people she had seen over the past several months were Smith and his men.

"A young cowboy stopped in the saloon in Cheyenne where I was having a drink. While having a drink together, he told me you were living up here alone. I figured it might be a good idea for me to come up this way and see if what he told me was true."

"It is true. My husband was murdered," she said softly.

"Murdered?"

"Yes. He was beaten to death by some men and left out in the woods to die. When I found him, I also found the two horses we used to pull our wagon were gone. They killed him and took our horses," she said, growing angrier with each minute.

"I take it from the sound of your voice you either have a pretty good idea who killed your husband and stole your horses, or you actually know who did it."

"Oh yes. I know who did it. It was Wilbur Smith and his ranch hands," she said sharply. "He has been trying to get me off my ranch ever since he murdered my husband."

"In what way?"

"First of all, Smith tried to buy our ranch from my husband, but he wouldn't sell it to him. The day after my husband was murdered, he came to see me to get me to leave. I told him I would never sell it to him then ran him off at the point of my shotgun. Then he had one of his men deliver a letter that simply read, 'GET OUT'.

"After that I shot Smith while he was on my ranch. He was sitting on his horse at the edge of the woods. Unfortunately, I didn't do anything more than wound him a little, which I'm sure did nothing more than make him mad."

Frank just looked at her and listened. The more she told him about what had been happening at her valley ranch, the more he thought she was probably right. Although he didn't know Smith personally, he had heard enough about him to know what kind of man he was. He was the kind that if he wanted her ranch, he was not about to let her keep it even if it meant killing her. As Frank saw it, there was only one thing he could do, and that was to help her keep her ranch.

"That's an interesting story," he said thoughtfully.

"It's no story," she said with a hint of anger in her voice. "It's what happened here over the past several months."

"I didn't mean it like that," he said as he looked into her eyes. "It's just that it might explain why I was shot not too far from your ranch. It would be my guess someone didn't want me to get here, probably so you would have no one to help you."

"Oh, I'm sorry," she said.

"It's okay, I understand."

"It will be hard for just the two of us to fight them. And right now, you are in no condition to start a war with the likes of Smith," she said, but almost wishing she had not said it.

"You are right, but we have a little time to prepare. If we get another foot or so of snow, it will keep them at bay for a few days, and hopefully, I will be in better shape by that time to help you if he should attack you," he said with a smile.

"At least for the next couple of days we will be able to get some rest, but once the snow melts it will be hard to fight them off," Susan said.

"We'll have to form a plan on how we will defend the ranch, and how we will attack them," he said with a smile."

"ATTACK THEM? Are you crazy?"

"I sure hope not. I have been in many fights with Indians and some white men. I was an officer during the Civil War. I learned when you're outnumbered, the best thing to do is to do what they least expect you to do. In this case, I would think the last thing Smith would expect you to do is attack him on his own land," he said with a grin. "We also have an advantage in the fact he doesn't know I'm here."

Susan just looked at him. It took her a minute or so, but she began to understand him a little. He was a bounty hunter and he was going to do whatever it took to make things right.

"What do we do now?" Susan asked having at least partially accepted the idea of the two of them defending the valley ranch from Smith.

"I think the best thing for us to do is to get some rest while we can," he said. "We can discuss what we are going to do when the weather gets better, and I have a better idea of what I will be able to do."

Susan looked at him for a moment, then stood up and leaned over him, carefully raising his head up a little to take the pillow out from under his head. She then pulled the quilt up over him and tucked him in.

"Goodnight. We'll talk again in the morning," she said with a smile, then blew out the lantern.

She stoked the fire before sitting down in her chair. She looked over at Frank as she pulled her quilt over her. He seemed to be asleep already. She closed her eyes and thought about the man lying in her bed before she drifted off to sleep.

It was still dark in the small cabin when Susan woke. She glanced over at the bed and found Frank sleeping. As she looked at him, she thought about what he had said yesterday about attacking Smith. It seemed risky, but then she had no idea what he really meant by "attacking" him. Was he thinking about an attack in the sense of going to Smith's ranch and fighting him there? Did he really mean to take the fight directly to Smith, to his ranch? Maybe he had something a little more subtle in mind, like causing a bit of confusion in Smith's mind, something that would make him less aggressive and less willing to attack her.

The more she thought about taking the fight to Smith, the more it caused her to wonder if they really could take the fight to him. Frank was certainly in no condition to take on Smith, or anyone else for that matter, at least for now. She doubted he would be ready for such a fight even if the snow lasted for a week, which was not likely this time of year. Early snows very often melted away in just a few days.

With that thought in mind, Susan got up from her chair and walked over to the window. She pulled the curtain back and looked outside. She just stared at the sight. There was at least two and a half to three feet of snow, and the sky was a dull gray as if it was ready to drop more in the valley. She could not remember ever seeing so much snow, but then she had only been in the valley for just over five months. It was her first winter in the valley. In Chicago she could only see for a short distance from the windows of the building which didn't allow her to see very much when it snowed. Her thoughts were suddenly disturbed by Frank.

"How's it look out there?" Frank asked from the bed.

"It looks wonderful. There has to be at least two and half to three feet of snow, and it looks like it might snow again."

Frank didn't miss the excitement in her voice. It made him feel a little better, too. He knew the more snow they had now, the longer he would have for his injuries to heal. However, he was well aware of the length of time it would take him to heal enough to put up a good fight. He also knew the heavy snow would give him time to figure out what he was going to do. His thoughts were suddenly disturbed by the sound of Susan's voice.

"Are you ready for something to eat?"

"Yes," he said as he looked at her.

Susan fixed breakfast for them. After they had finished eating, Susan went about her morning chores. She bundled up in her heavy coat, strapped a gun around her waist then put on her boots before leaving the cabin. She went to the barn where she gathered the eggs from the few chickens she still had, then fed the chickens in the barn. She cleaned the stalls and took care of the horses. When she was done, she returned to the cabin. As she came into the cabin, she glanced over at Frank to see if he needed anything. She found that he was resting peacefully.

# CHAPTER EIGHT

Time passed slowly. As the days passed, Frank gradually grew stronger; and he was able to move around in the bed with less pain. His wounds healed slowly, but they were getting better.

The weather eventually cleared and the sun shined on the valley once again. The temperatures at night were below freezing, but during the day were just barely above freezing causing the snow to melt slowly.

Frank and Susan spent a good part of the day talking about the area. Frank wanted to know everything he could about the valley and the surrounding hills. He wanted to know if there was any other way in or out of the valley, other than the narrow canyon his horse had used to get him to her cabin. He questioned her about the surrounding hills and if there were any trails in them that might lead over the ridge behind the barn.

"There are several buffalo trails that meander around in the rocky hills behind the cabin, but I don't know where they go," Susan said. "My husband said some of them went over the ridge to a valley north of us. I think he might have done some hunting back in there, but he didn't say much about it."

"I think Smith's ranch is south and west of here," Frank said thoughtfully. "Did he say anything about any trails that might go south or west from here?"

"Not really. He said he didn't explore them because they might lead to Smith's ranch, and he didn't want to run into Smith or any of his ranch hands while he was out there alone. I don't think he knew for sure if any of the trails went in that direction. He did say there were several deer trails and a buffalo trail that might go toward Smith's ranch, but he never checked them out to see where they went."

"We might want to check them out as soon as possible," he said as he thought about what she had said. "We might find one that would get us close to Smith's ranch and hopefully his ranch house without him being able to see us."

"Are you still thinking about attacking him at his ranch?" she asked, a little afraid of what his answer might be.

"Yes, but only if it offers us a way to make a clean escape."

It was getting late in the afternoon and Frank had been in bed for a week. When Susan was not looking, he had tried to do a few light exercises in the hope of keeping from getting too stiff and weak. He looked at her as she was standing in front of the dry sink fixing their dinner. He reflected on his time here in her cabin.

They were using first names now, and he had been thinking of her a lot. He couldn't help but think about her. Even in a simple cotton dress, she was a beautiful young woman with a smooth complexion, soft blond hair and beautiful blue eyes. He hadn't missed the fact that under the simple cotton dress was a woman with a very nice figure.

She was also a caring person. During the time they had spent together, she had bathed him, fed him, and redressed his wounds. She had continued to sleep in a chair which he was sure was not all that comfortable for her.

Frank thought many times about asking her if she would like to sleep in the bed. After all, it was big enough for the two of them. Maybe it was time to bring it up. He had seen her stretch to get the stiffness out of her back when she would first get up in the morning. There was little doubt in his mind she was not getting any real rest.

"Susan," he said in almost a whisper.

She turned, looked at him and smiled then asked, "What is it?"

"I was wondering, ah, well, I was thinking that you, ah, you might sleep better if you slept in the bed."

The smile left her face as she looked at him. She wasn't sure what he really meant. It wasn't that she hadn't thought about sleeping in the bed with him, but what was he really saying?

"I'm sorry. I should make it clear what I mean. I've noticed you seem to be getting stiff and not sleeping very well in the chair. I just thought you might sleep better if you could lie down on the bed to sleep."

She just looked at him. The feelings that were running through her mind caused her some confusion. She had to fight the thoughts she had about sleeping with him and wanting him to hold her close to make her feel safe. She also had to fight her feelings of being so lonely.

"I have to admit that I do miss sleeping in a bed, but are you sure it's a good idea?" she asked as she looked at him.

"I would like you to help me get up," he said without answering her question. "I need to move around a little. If it goes well, I could sleep in the chair for a night or two so you could get some real rest," he offered as a way to make it easier for her to accept his idea of her sleeping in the bed.

It struck her that he was just trying to help her get some rest. For some reason she could not explain, even to herself, she felt a little disappointed, but shook that thought from her mind. It was obvious to her that he was trying to be a gentleman, and showing that he was concerned for her well-being.

"Do you think you're ready to get up?"

"Yes, I think so. We won't know unless I try."

"Okay," she said as she put down the knife she had been using to prepare their dinner.

Susan walked over to the bed. She hesitated to lift up the quilt because she was well aware of the fact he was naked, and had been since she first bathed him. She lifted the quilt then helped him sit up. As soon as he was sitting up, she wrapped the quilt around his shoulders in an effort to keep him warm, and to cover him. She had not only seen him naked, but she noticed the pain on his face as he sat up. She wondered if he was really ready to get up.

"Are you going to help me up?" he asked, disturbing her thoughts.

"Yes," she said then leaned down in front of him and slipped her arms under his arms.

"Ready?" she asked looking into his eyes.

"Yes," he said as he reached out and put his hands on her shoulders then girtted his teeth in anticipation of pain.

He pulled himself up as she helped lift him. He felt a little dizzy and wrapped his arms around her neck and leaned against her for support. He felt her body against him as he leaned against her and took a couple of deep breaths.

Susan could feel him against her as she wrapped her arms around his narrow waist to support him. It seemed as if it had been an eternity since she had held a man or been held by a man, let alone being held by a man who was naked. She looked up at him. She could see the pain in his eyes and the paleness of his face, and thought it might be best if he lay back down.

"Are you all right?" she asked.

"Just give me a minute to catch my breath."

She stood there holding him in her arms while he tried to catch his breath. She could feel the warmth of his body through her dress. Her thoughts of how good it felt to have a man hold her were disturbed when Frank spoke.

"I think I can stand now."

Susan looked at his face. The color seemed to have returned to his face. She slowly took her arms from around him and carefully stepped back, staying close enough to grab him if it looked like he was going to fall. She stood back and looked at him. She couldn't help but notice his broad chest and narrow waist.

"I could sure use something to wear," he said as he looked down at her.

She suddenly realized the quilt that had been covering him had fallen off him. She turned red with embarrassment and looked away.

"I'll get your clothes. Will you be all right if I leave you for a minute?"

"Yes, I think so."

Susan turned and went over to the pegs on the wall on the other side of the bed and retrieved his pants and shirt she had cleaned while he was resting from his injuries. She quickly returned to him.

"I'll need some help," he said.

Susan didn't say anything, she simple let him lean against her while she helped him get dressed. Once he was dressed, she helped him walk around the cabin. She led him around with his arm over her shoulder. When he was tired, which didn't take but a few minutes, she helped him sit down in her chair. She covered him with a quilt, then returned to preparing dinner without saying a word.

While she prepared dinner, her thoughts were of Frank. Was he married? Did he have a family somewhere? If he wasn't married, did he have a sweetheart? It wasn't long before she realized she was just standing there staring at the pan in front of her. He was consuming her thoughts. A tear came to her eye as she realized she was lonely and desperate for the love and affection of a man.

She also realized she needed to pull herself together and get her thoughts directed toward saving her ranch. He had not done anything that should make her feel the way she did.

It was time to get her feelings under control and keep them that way.

When it was time for dinner, Susan helped Frank to the table. When dinner was over, they sat at the table to talk. Susan wanted to know more about him.

"I've been meaning to ask you, do you have a family somewhere, maybe in Custer City?" she asked.

"No. I took a job with the Deadwood to Cheyenne Stagecoach Company to protect a gold shipment. The job simply ended in Cheyenne. When the cowboy in Cheyenne told me that you might be here all alone, and I had nothing else to do and no place to go; I decided to come out here and make sure you were doing all right. If something happened to me, no one would miss me," he said.

"Certainly, there would be someone?"

"Nope. No wife, no girlfriend, no children, no one. Like you, I have no one. I happen to know you were a mail-order bride."

"How is it you know that?"

"Even out here where people often live miles from their nearest neighbor and don't see anyone for weeks or months at a time, news still travels pretty fast. Word gets around out here. Once the postman knows something, it gets around," he said with a slight grin."

"Why is it no one knew I was alone and that my husband was murdered?"

"I think the cowboy who told me you were living alone knew a lot more than he was telling me. If I had to guess, he not only knew you were here alone; but he was probably involved in some way with the death of your husband."

"You think he might have been one of those who murdered my husband?" she asked.

"Could be, but I seriously doubt he did any of the beating, but he was probably there. I'm sure the reason he left the area was he didn't like what happened and couldn't stomach it. I doubt he would want to tell anyone that he was there. If he did, he would probably be arrested, tried and hung."

Susan looked at him for a moment, then stood up and went over to the dry sink. She began washing the dishes from dinner, but suddenly stopped and leaned against the counter. Her eyes filled with tears as she thought about what had happened to her husband.

Frank looked at her. He was sure she was crying, but had no idea what he could do to make her feel better. He slowly got up, walked across the room and stood behind her. He reached out and touched her shoulder.

As soon as Susan felt Frank touch her on the shoulder, she turned around and leaned against him. She wrapped her arms around him and put her head on his chest then cried openly. She felt him wrap her in his arms and hold her to him. For the first time in a long time, she felt safe, and that there was someone in the world who cared about her.

After a few minutes, she pushed herself away from him and looked up at him. She could see the concern he had for her on his face. The more she looked at him the more she wanted to kiss him.

"Are you all right?" Frank asked.

"Yes," she replied in a whisper. "Jacob wanted so much to make a home for me here."

"I'm sure he did," was all Frank could think to say.

"I would like to go to bed now. Do you mind?"

"No. I'll sleep in the chair," Frank said.

Frank let go of her, then returned to the chair and sat down. He closed his eyes but didn't go right to sleep. He could hear Susan moving around in the cabin. He heard the bed springs squeak a little when she sat down on the bed. It wasn't long before he could hear her slow steady breathing. She had fallen asleep.

It was not so easy for Frank to fall asleep. He could remember the feel of her warm body against him when she held him, and the way she looked at him when she cared for his wounds. He would never forget the way he felt when she was in his arms. He had had the desire to kiss her, but didn't think it was a good idea.

Thoughts of being with her after he was done there didn't help him get to sleep, but finally sleep came.

# CHAPTER NINE

When morning came, Susan woke and turned to see if Frank was still sleeping in the chair. She sat up quickly when she saw the chair was empty. The panic she felt caused her heart to race and her breath to catch. She didn't know what to think, or where he might have gone.

She stood up and looked around the cabin. As she looked around the room, the first thing she saw was Frank's coat was missing from the hook near the door. She ran to the window and looked outside. There were tracks in the snow indicating he had gone outside. From the window, she followed the line of tracks that led toward the barn. Her first thought was he had left, but where did he go? Had he left her to fend for herself? She couldn't believe he would do that to her. Did he get his horse and head for Smith's ranch? That didn't seem likely, either. First of all, he was in no condition to take on anyone. Secondly, he was not ready to be riding a horse over such rough terrain, and finally, the snow was still too deep for a horse to take him anywhere.

Not knowing what else to do, she slipped on her boots and wrapped her heavy coat around her, then grabbed a gun and headed for the barn. She stepped in his tracks making it easier for her to walk through the deep snow. The only tracks she saw were his tracks to the barn. She didn't see any tracks from a horse or from his boots leaving the barn. When she got to the barn door, she slowly opened it and stepped inside. She was not sure what she would find.

Frank was standing in the stall next to his horse slowly rubbing the horse's neck and talking softly to it. She could see through the slats in the stall that the horse was eating. She walked up to the stall.

"You scared me half to death," she said with a bit of anger in her voice. "You're in no shape to be caring for the horses."

Frank turned and looked at her. He could see by the look on her face that she was angry with him for causing her to worry.

"I'm sorry I worried you. I didn't mean to. I didn't want to wake you, and I was sure the horses needed to be fed."

"I hope you are not planning on going for a ride. If you do, you will probably open your wounds."

"No. I have no intention of riding a horse. I know that I'm not ready to ride yet, but I will be soon," he said.

"What makes you so sure?"

"I have to be ready to ride in a day or so if we are going to take on Smith before he attacks us here," he said.

"Are both of the horses fed and watered?" she asked.

"Yes."

"Then you best come inside. I'll fix breakfast. You have to eat if you want to regain your strength."

Susan turned around and started out of the barn without waiting to see if he would follow her. Susan took a deep breath as she walked toward the cabin. Frank not being in the cabin when she woke had caused her a great deal of concern. It was a relief that he had not reinjured himself by doing too much too soon. In fact, it was a relief to find he had not left her.

Once inside the cabin, Susan immediately went to the other side of the bed and got dressed. Frank came in just as she finished dressing. She began fixing breakfast for them.

Frank sat down at the table and watched her. He took his time before he spoke to her. He knew she was angry with him, and the last thing he wanted to do was to make matters worse by saying something stupid.

"I figure I have a couple of days before the snow melts enough to allow travel," he said hoping it would not make her more upset with him.

Susan turned and looked at him for a moment before she spoke, "It will take longer than that for the snow to melt in the narrow canyon leading in here. The sun doesn't get into the bottom of the canyon this time of year."

"I wasn't thinking about the canyon, but I am hoping Smith is thinking about it. The snow on the buffalo trail that runs behind the barn and leads in the direction of Smith's ranch is not nearly as deep," he said. "I think we will be able to get close to his ranch house without being seen by going over the ridge."

"I take it you have a plan," Susan said as she set two plates on the table.

"I do, and it requires your help," he said with a grin.

Frank didn't say anything more about his plan until breakfast was on the table and Susan had sat down. As he explained what he had in mind, they ate breakfast. It was not a very complicated plan, but it sounded like a good one, one that just might work.

After breakfast, Frank and Susan cleaned up the dishes before they discussed his plan in detail. One of the major elements of Frank's plan required him to be able to ride a horse. In order for him to do that, he needed to have his wounds bandaged, and they needed to be wrapped tight enough to prevent his wounds from opening so they wouldn't bleed. He also needed to have enough flexibility to allow him to move about with a minimum amount of pain.

Susan understood what had to be done. She gathered several pieces of cloth, then took the dressings off his wounds to make sure they were healing well. Satisfied his wounds were healing well, and he had not caused them to reopen, she replaced the dressings. She then took a long piece of cloth and wrapped it around his body several times, making it tight enough to give him good support, but not so tight it would be difficult for him to breath.

Satisfied that the wound in his side was protected from further injury as best it could be, she took a second piece of cloth and wrapped his leg. Again, she checked it to make sure he could stand without too much discomfort and still be able to bend his knee a little and move his leg enough to get on and off a horse without hurting himself too much.

Once she was done, he stood up and moved around the room. It was still painful to walk on the leg and bending at the waist hurt a bit, too, but he smiled at her after walking around the table two or three times and bending over a little several times.

"I think this will be all right if I don't do too much, too quickly," he said.

"I don't know if it will keep you from opening up your wounds," Susan said with a look of concern on her face.

"Well, I guess it will have to do. I don't see we can wait much longer. If we wait too long, we will have to fight him here. I would prefer not to do that, at least at first."

"We might still have to fight him here if he figures out how we got to his place," Susan said.

"True, but if we attack him at his ranch when he least expects it, he will be a little more cautious about coming over the ridge and attacking us here. It will also give us time to get ready for him."

"I guess you're right," she said, still not sure attacking Smith was the best thing to do. "I think you should move around with the tight bandages on for a little while just in case we have them too tight."

"I don't think they are too tight, but that's still a good idea," Frank said as he began walking around the cabin. As small as the cabin was, about the only place he could walk was around the table. He first walked one way, then turned around and walked the other way around the table.

"Don't overdo it," Susan reminded him. "In a little while, I'll take the bandages off to make sure you haven't broken open your wounds."

After an hour of walking around inside the cabin, and going out to the barn in the heavy snow a few times, Frank sat down at the table. He looked a little tired, but that was to be expected since he had lost a lot of blood, and it was the first time he had been up and moving around in over a week.

"How are you feeling?" Susan asked.

"I'm doing okay, but I'm a little tired," Frank said.

"Just don't overdo it."

"While I was outside, I did a little looking around. I didn't see any tracks that would tell us if there is someone around. That's a good sign, but I saw several fresh buffalo tracks and deer tracks that tells me the animals are starting to move around again," Frank said.

"I take it you think we should make our move soon?"

"I think we should put our plan into action in the morning. We will start out as soon as it is light enough to see where we are going."

"Okay, then we should get a good night's rest tonight," she said.

"Yes," he agreed, then got up and walked over to the chair he had used last night and started laying out a quilt.

"What are you doing? You need your rest. Take the bed, you'll rest better there," she insisted.

"You need your rest, too. We could share the bed," Frank said as he watched for her reaction.

Susan stood there and looked at him. His suggestion was something she had not expected. He had been in her cabin for over a week and had been a perfect gentleman.

The idea of sleeping in the same bed with him was not a new thought to her. She had thought about it several times during the time she had been sleeping in the chair while he slept in her bed recovering from his injuries. She had blamed her thoughts of sharing the bed with him on her loneliness and the fear she had of being alone. Now that he was able to get around she seemed uncertain about it.

"I promise to be a gentleman and not bother you so you can get some well needed sleep," he said when she didn't respond to his suggestion.

Susan thought about his statement, then wondered if it was him that she should be concerned with. She had already had thoughts of what it would be like to be held in his arms, and to sleep in her bed with him. She had been able to control those thoughts, but could she continue to control them if she was lying close beside him.

"Okay," Susan finally agreed, but not without a hint of nervousness in her voice.

"It is dark out. Maybe we should get ready for bed," Frank said.

"Yes. That is probably a good idea," she said feeling a little nervous about it.

Without any hesitation, Frank walked around to the side of the bed closest to the wall. He sat down on the edge of the bed and took off his clothes, then lifted the covers and climbed under the quilt. He then turned over on his side facing the wall with his back to Susan.

Susan heard him get into bed. She had been standing next to the window and looking outside. There were a lot of thoughts going through her mind. They were all about the wisdom of sleeping with him. She took a deep breath then turned and looked at the bed. Frank was in the bed with his back to her. It seemed he was trying to make it easier for her.

Susan blew out the lantern then moved closer to the bed. The only light in the cabin was from the soft glow of the fire in the fireplace. Keeping her eyes on Frank, she undressed and slipped into her night gown, a simple white cotton gown that covered her from her neck to her feet. She lifted the covers and slipped into the bed, quickly covering herself. She lay on her back and pulled the quilt up to her neck then turned her head and looked over at Frank. He was still lying on his side facing away from her.

Susan lay quietly on her back looking up at the ceiling. She had not been in a bed with a man since before her husband had been killed. It felt strange to be in a bed with a man now. It wasn't that she was afraid of him, but it was what she was thinking. Her mind was filled with all sorts of thoughts, thoughts of wanting a man to hold her in his arms, to being nervous about having a man in her bed, to actually liking the idea of having a man in her bed. All the thoughts racing through her head made it hard for her to go to sleep, but sleep finally did come to her.

Susan didn't know how long she had been asleep when she felt a movement next to her. She was lying on her side with her back toward Frank. She opened her eyes only to find the cabin was dark and she could not see anything, but she could feel the warmth of his breath on the back of her neck. She suddenly realized that Frank had rolled over on his other side and was now facing her, and he was very close to her.

She lay quietly and listened. From the sound of his breathing, he was still asleep. Susan's mind wanted him to curl up against her, hold her against him and make her feel loved, something she had not had time to feel in the short time she had been married to Jacob.

Frank had come to make sure she was not in any danger, not to fall in love with her. He had found she was in danger, but once the danger was gone, she was sure he would leave and return to where he came from once again leaving her alone. In her mind there was nothing she could do about that. She closed her eyes again and slowly drifted off to sleep.

# CHAPTER TEN

As the sunshine began to shine through the window of the small cabin, Susan woke and found herself lying very close to Frank. She could feel the warmth of his body making it obvious that he was very close to her. She had to admit to herself that she liked the feeling it gave her, but she also had to admit she was sure that it would not last.

They had things to do, and it was time to get up and get started. Susan moved away from Frank and sat up on the edge of the bed. She looked over her shoulder and found Frank looking at her.

"I think we should get up," Susan said. "I need to get dressed. Would you mind turning over?"

Frank didn't reply, he simply turned over and looked at the wall while Susan took off her night gown and slipped into a man's shirt that had once belonged to her husband. She also put on her husband's pants that she had cut down to fit her, knowing today was not going to be a good day for a dress. Wearing men's clothes did nothing to hide the fact she was a woman. However, the men's clothes would be more practical for what the day was sure to bring.

As soon as she was dressed, she turned and looked at Frank. He was sitting up on the edge of the bed facing the wall.

"You can turn around now," Susan said. "I'll start breakfast while you dress."

"What about the bandages? I'll need help with them."

"Oh. I'll help you with them first."

Susan walked over to the bed and knelt down in front of him. She wrapped his leg the same way she had wrapped it the day before. When she looked up, she found him watching her. Just the fact he was looking at her made her nervous. She stood up in front of him.

"You will need to stand up," she said.

Frank stood up. She took the long piece of cloth she had wrapped him with the day before and began wrapping it around him again. She had it around him twice when she pulled it up snug. The tugging on the cloth caught Frank a little off balance causing him to fall forward. He reached out and put his hands on Susan's shoulders to help regain his balance.

Susan quickly straightened up and grabbed him by his waist to support him. She suddenly found herself with his arms wrapped around her. She also had her arms wrapped around him. The feel of his body against her caused her heart to race and her breath to catch. She didn't move for a moment or two before she let go of him and stepped back.

"Are you okay?" she asked, her voice showing she was still a little shaken.

"Yes. I'm sorry. I lost my balance for a second."

Susan didn't respond, she simply began to wrap the cloth around his waist again. As soon as she had it secured, Susan went over to the counter and began fixing breakfast while Frank got dressed. Nothing more was said about the incident, but it continued to occupy Susan's mind.

They ate breakfast, then Frank went out to the barn and saddled the horses while Susan cleaned up the dishes. When she was done, she sat down at the table and wrote out the message Frank had suggested she write to leave for Smith to find.

After finishing the message, she put on a holster and checked the gun to make sure it was ready to use. After putting on a coat, she picked up the rifle she had next to the door then went out to the barn. Entering the barn, she saw Frank putting a saddle on her horse, his horse was already saddled and ready to go. She walked up to Frank and looked at him.

"How are you feeling?" she asked, a look of concern on her face.

"I'm okay," he said as he looked at her. "Are you ready?"

"Yes," she said, but didn't sound too convincing.

"You ride out the front of the barn then go up into the woods and onto the buffalo trail. Stay on the trail, or as close to it as possible. I'll go out the back of the barn and ride well off the trail so if you are followed after our attack on them they will have only one set of tracks to follow. It will also put me in a position to cover your retreat if anyone should come after you."

"Okay," she said softly.

"You know what you are to do when we find the ranch house?"

"Yes. I'm to fire a shot at the front door of the ranch house then get out of there as fast as I can."

"Yes, but don't forget to leave the message where they can find it before you shoot. It would help if they saw you leave it, but the letter will certainly let them know it was you attacking them."

"But will they think it is me dressed like this?"

"They will know it's you. If nothing else, they will know that horse. There isn't another black and white paint like it around here. The message will also let them know who shot at the ranch house," Frank assured her.

"Okay," she said, then turned toward her horse.

Susan got up in the saddle, then rode out of the barn. She looked back in time to see Frank close the barn door. She turned her horse then headed for the buffalo trail back in the woods. Looking around she didn't see Frank. It caused her to suddenly feel very much alone. Even though she was sure he was watching her from deeper in the woods, she was still very nervous. She wondered if it was the way soldiers felt when they were going into battle. It seemed like a strange thought for her to have, but it did feel like she was going into battle.

The ride along the buffalo trail was slow going. The trail was not only difficult for the horse, but it was hard on the rider. It wound around and between trees, as well as going up and down the steep sides of the hills making it hard to stay in the saddle at times. Plus, there were places where the snow had drifted and it was still fairly deep, making it hard for the horse. With the light snow cover on the trail, there were loose rocks hidden under the snow making the footing for the horse difficult at times. She tried to make it easier on the horse by riding alongside the trail where the horse could get better footing.

It was almost mid-morning by the time Susan came to a place where she could see out onto an open pasture while still remaining in the woods. She stopped her horse and looked around. She was not only looking for where she should go from there, but she was looking for Frank and his dapple gray horse. She saw neither of them. What she did see was a large open pasture with what looked like almost two hundred head of cattle on it. It didn't appear as there had been as much snow in the pasture as they had gotten at the cabin. It crossed her mind that some of those cattle might belong to her.

She knew Smith's ranch was large, but she didn't know where the ranch house was located. Susan suddenly heard something off to her left. She turned to see what had made the noise. It took her a moment or so before she could see Frank sitting on his horse at least fifty yards away in among the trees. The dapple gray was almost invisible with the snow, pine needles and trees in the area. Frank was pointing toward something in front and off to her right a little. She turned and looked where he was pointing. In the distance, she could make out what looked like a chimney just barely sticking up from behind a hill. There was a thin line of smoke coming from it.

She turned back and looked at Frank, he was motioning for her to turn and go back into the woods then work her way around the hill. She turned her horse, then looked at Frank. She signaled the direction she thought he wanted her to go. When he responded by waving his hand above his head to let her know she was correct, she started working her way along the edge of the woods.

Moving along rather slowly while staying inside yet close to the edge of the woods, she was able to keep an eye on the chimney. The further along she got, the more of the ranch house came into view, first the roof and then enough of the building to know it was the ranch house.

When she had a clear view of the entire front porch from the woods, Susan stopped and got off her horse. After tying the horse to a tree, she walked to a large tree at the edge of the woods. She stood behind the tree while she looked around. She looked down at the ranch house trying to decide where she should leave the message and how she was going to get away.

It didn't take her long to figure out where to leave the message. She found a couple of small rocks and picked them up and then crouched down as she moved to a nearby wooden fence post just outside the woods. She placed the rocks on the top of the fence post, then using the rocks like bookends, she placed the message between the rocks so it could be seen clearly from the front porch of the ranch house. If anyone came that way, there was little doubt they would see the message. She immediately returned to where she had left her horse.

Standing next to her horse, she pulled her rifle from the scabbard and levered a round into the chamber. Looking around, she found a nearby tree with a branch that would provide her with a place to support the rifle while she fired at the house, as well as provide her with a little protection. She placed the gun on the branch of the tree next to the trunk and took aim at the front porch of the ranch house.

On the front porch of the ranch house was a large clay pot that appeared to have dried flowers still in it. It was setting on the table only a couple of feet from the front door. Susan took careful aim at the pot then slowly pulled the trigger. The rifle made a loud bang and the pot exploded scattering pieces of it all over the porch along with the dirt that was inside it.

It was only a matter of seconds before the front door of the ranch house flew open and Wilbur Smith stepped out on the porch with a pistol in his hand. The first thing he saw was the shattered pot and the dirt scattered all over the porch. He looked around to see where the shot had come from, but didn't see anyone.

Susan took careful aim again from her place on the hill at the edge of the woods. She slowly pulled the trigger and fired a second shot hitting the door handle of the front door right next to Smith. Smith jumped off the porch and ducked down behind the watering trough.

"Give me back my cattle," Susan yelled.

When Susan saw several ranch hands starting to come out of the bunkhouse with guns in their hands, she quickly turned and ran to her horse. She jumped into the saddle, kicked her horse in the ribs and took off, heading deeper into the woods as fast as the horse could carry her. She didn't once look back, but she heard several shots, a couple of bullets hit trees near her as she rode away.

It was only a few seconds before she was deep enough in the woods that she would be out of sight of anyone at the ranch house, but she didn't slow down. The only thing she could think about was getting as far away as she could, as quickly as possible.

Once she was back on the same buffalo trail she had used to get to the Smith ranch, she had to slow down. To run her horse over the trail could mean almost certain injury to the horse. If it stumbled on a rock or in a small hole, it could not only break its leg, but it could throw her off. She could not afford to lose the horse, and she certainly would not want to be caught away from her ranch on foot by Smith or any of his men.

Susan hadn't gone very far when she heard several more shots from behind her. They were not being fired at her as she was too far away. She wondered if Frank had gotten into a gunfight with some of Smith's ranch hands. He had said he would cover her escape, and it sounded like that was what he was doing.

Susan looked back over her shoulder as she thought about what might have happened back there. She found herself thinking about Frank, and hoping he was all right. She worried about his injuries and hoped they were not causing him any problems. She was also worried about him receiving any new injuries.

It was just a few minutes after the noon hour when she returned to her valley ranch. Susan had followed the buffalo trail all the way back, just like they had planned. She immediately led her horse into the barn, and took the saddle off it. She quickly rubbed the horse down and gave him a hand full of grain and some hay. She then returned to the cabin to wait for Frank.

Time passed by slowly, each minute seemed like an hour. Susan continued to watch out the window with a rifle in one hand and her shotgun close by. If Frank had been shot while she escaped, it would not be long before Smith's men would be coming to burn her out, and possibly kill her. She would have to be ready for an attack.

Susan gathered up as much of the ammunition as she had in the house and stacked it next to the door. She then lined up the guns on the shelf near the door where she could get at them easily.

Suddenly she heard the sound of a horse coming down the hill behind the barn. She could not see who it was from the cabin. Susan ran for the barn with her rifle in hand. From there she could see out the back window of the barn for anyone coming down off the hill. She was ready should any of Smith's men be coming that way.

Her heart skipped a beat when she saw Frank coming down off the hill. He seemed to be slumped over his saddle. She was sure he was injured again. The only thing she didn't know was if his injury was one he started out with or if he had been shot again. She set the rifle against the door and ran out to him. As she grabbed the horse by his bridle, Frank sat up and smiled down at her. It was obvious he was hurting even though he was smiling at her.

"Well, I think we started us a war," Frank said.

"Are you okay?" Susan said with a worried look on her face.

"Yah. I'm hurtin' a bit, but not because I was shot again. Riding a horse at a full run sure does shake a guy up. Help me down."

She led the horse into the barn, then held her arms out as Frank started to get out of the saddle. Once he was standing on the ground, she supported him as she walked him over to a bench next to a stall. She helped him sit down to give him a chance to rest a bit before helping him to the cabin.

"I heard a couple of shots after I was well away from Smith's ranch house. Did you fire them?"

"Yes. There were a couple of ranch hands that started up the hill where you had tied your horse. I discourage them from following you. They were just nervous and wanted to make sure you had left the area."

Once Frank had caught his breath, Susan again helped him to his feet. She had him put his arm over her shoulders while she led him to the cabin. Once inside the cabin, she helped him out of his coat and took him to the bed. She had him sit down on the bed as gently as she could, then took his shirt off. Susan carefully unwrapped the cloth from around his waist and removed the dressing. The wound to his side was inflamed a little, but it had not broken open.

"It's not looking good, but you didn't break it open," she said as she looked up at his face. "How does your leg feel?"

"My leg feels fine. It's just my side that hurts."

"You best get some rest. I'll keep an eye out for Smith and any of his men. I probably left a trail right back to here."

"I doubt he will come here right away. We stung him pretty good. Right know he is probably confused and will need a little time to plan his next move," Frank said. "Where is the best place to keep an eye on your cabin and barn?"

"I would think it would be from the loft in the barn. From there I can see out in front of the cabin and the trails into the hills out behind which we used to get to his place."

"Help me out to the barn."

"You can't go out there. You need to rest. I'll go watch."

"Okay, I won't argue with you. Wear something warm. It's going to get cold tonight. Call if you see them."

"I will, but you need to rest."

Frank nodded that he understood, and he was not about to argue with her. He knew he would not be much good in a fight right now. He did need to rest before he was in another fight.

Susan bundled up and took a couple of quilts with her to the barn. She took care of Frank's horse before going up into the loft. She found a place in the loft where she could see most of the area around the barn and cabin, then settled in to keep watch.

The hour grew late as Susan sat next to the loft door watching for anything that might cause them harm. Her muscles tightened when she thought she heard what sounded like a large animal moving among the trees. She listened very carefully in the hope of seeing it before she was spotted.

Suddenly, an elk moved slowly out of the woods then turned and walked along the edge of the woods. It was followed by twenty to thirty more elk.

Susan smiled at the sight of all the elk slowly walking out of the woods. The sight of all the elk gave her hope there would be no attack from Smith and his men tonight. The elk would not be moving along so slowly if there was anyone around. Secondly, the elk had come down out of the hills on the buffalo trail that she had used to go to and from Smith's ranch. She was sure so many elk would have wiped out her tracks, but she knew it didn't really matter. Smith already knew who had attacked him.

With the lateness of the hour it was getting dark, too dark to be able to follow tracks or to even move around in the woods with any degree of safety. There was no moon out because the clouds had moved in during the evening. Her last sight of the clouds hinted that it might snow again. Susan was sure with the change of weather and the elk passing through, there was little to no chance Smith would be coming for revenge tonight.

Suddenly it began to snow. It started out rather slowly, but soon picked up and was coming down hard. She smiled up at the dark sky and the large wet snowflakes as they fell. The snow began to build up rapidly on the edge of the open loft door. It would not be long before the snow would make it almost impossible to travel.

Susan closed the loft door, gathered up her quilts and returned to the cabin. When she opened the door, she was greeted by Frank with a pistol firmly gripped in his hand. He quickly put the gun down when he saw her enter.

"How are you feeling?" she asked as she set the rifle down next to the door.

"Not bad. In fact, a lot better now that it is snowing again."

"I don't think anyone will be traveling in this tonight. I thought I would come in and get warmed up, get something to eat and get some rest."

"Good idea."

Susan added a couple of logs to the fire, then prepared a dinner for them. It wasn't much, just a few eggs and a piece of meat, but it was enough.

After she cleaned up the dishes, Susan turned down the lantern, took off her clothing and put on her night gown. She then blew out the lantern, and laid down on the bed beside Frank. She felt comfortable in the bed with him, even if it still felt a little strange to have him in her bed. It didn't take any time at all for her to fall asleep. It had been a long and stressful day.

# CHAPTER ELEVEN

The attack on the Smith Ranch caused several minutes of total chaos for Smith and his ranch hands. Smith was feeling fear as he had never felt it before. For the first time in his life, he had been challenged. Smith had heard Mrs. McDonald yell out her demand. He had felt the splinters of wood hit him when the bullet struck the door only inches from him. He was scared, scared of losing everything he had built up over the years, and scared of losing his life.

After hearing the sounds of a horse leaving the area, Smith slowly rose up and looked over the top of the watering trough. When he didn't see anyone and was sure it was clear, he slowly stood up and brushed the snow from his clothes. He continued to look up the hill where the shots had come from, and where Mrs. McDonald had called out her demand.

He turned and looked toward the corner of the ranch house when he heard several of his ranch hands come running around the corner. The ranch hands had guns in their hands and were ready for a fight, but had no idea who they were to fight, where they were, or what was going on. They looked around as if confused, then looked to Smith for direction. Two of the ranch hands started up the hill, but were turned back by someone shooting at them.

"It was that damn woman," Smith shouted, his voice showing his anger. "She shot at me. Don't just stand there, do something."

"You want us to go after her?" Jesse asked.

Smith just looked up the hill where the shot had been fired from and where he had seen Mrs. McDonald for only a moment. He could not believe she had the nerve to shoot at him on his own property. In a way he admired her grit, but not so much that he was going to let her get away with it, and certainly not so much as to let her stay in the valley.

"No," Smith finally said as he thought about her. "I'm going to take the fight to her. She's goin' to wish she hadn't attacked me."

"Say, Mr. Smith, what's that up there, on top of that fence post?" Jesse asked as he pointed at the post.

"I don't see - -, I don't know. Go get it," he ordered, curious as to what was on the post.

Jesse looked at Smith, then started up the hill. He took his time as he moved carefully closer to the fence post. When he was almost in reach of the fence post, he stopped and looked around before he approached it. He held his gun firmly in his hand as his eyes kept moving as if he expected someone to be hanging around and was using the paper like bait in a trap. Not seeing anyone, he moved up to the fence post. He saw it was an envelope held upright between two rocks on top of the post.

After checking around to see if anyone might be just waiting to shoot at him, he grabbed the envelope while still looking around. He carefully backed away from the fence post for several yards before he turned around and ran back down the hill.

"Looks like she left ya a note," Jesse said as he held the envelope out to Smith.

Smith reached out and snatched the envelope from the foreman, but didn't bother to open it. He simply looked up the hill where she had yelled out her demand.

"If that damn woman thinks she can threaten me, she's got another think coming. She's not going to get away with it."

The foreman just looked at his boss. Jesse could see the anger on his face. He had never seen Smith so mad. He wondered what was going through his boss's mind. Jesse wondered if he really wanted to get involved in a war between his boss and the widow lady who was all alone. As much as he liked the job of foreman, and the pay, going after a woman just didn't seem right. He also didn't think that most people would find it right, either. In fact, he knew it wasn't right, and men had been hung for nothing more than hitting a woman. Smith was planning a lot more than simply hitting her.

As Smith looked up the hill, there was little doubt that he was fuming mad. He had just been attacked on his own front porch by a wisp of a woman who was making demands of him. He was not about to let a woman, any woman for that matter, make him do anything he didn't want to do.

"That damn woman is not going to get the best of me," he said out loud, but to himself. "I'll kill her."

"Did you say somethin', boss?" Jesse asked, knowing full well what his boss had said.

"Get the men together. I'm going to put a stop to her right now. I want that valley and I'm going to have it tonight."

"Excuse me, sir," Jesse said, hoping to get his boss to take a moment to think before he did something foolish, "but have you given any real thought to going after her?"

"What's there to think about?" Smith asked, giving his foreman an angry look.

"Do you really think she'd come here alone and make such a demand?"

"What are you getting at?"

"I have to wonder if she is really alone."

"Speak up. Do you know something? Have you or any of the men seen someone else around her place?"

"No, but a couple of the hands were shot at on their way up the hill to where she had been and near where she left the letter. One of them got hit by some bark off a tree that was hit by a bullet. The last time we saw her, she was makin' a run for it as fast as that horse of hers would go."

"So? What are you saying? You think someone was up there to make sure that she was covered while she ran back to her ranch?"

"I don't know, but think about this. Suppose there was someone else in the woods coverin' her as she left. Someone who would be there to make sure she got away safe and sound."

"None of the men have reported seeing anyone in the valley except for her," Smith reminded Jesse.

"That don't mean there's no one else around. After all, we ain't been watchin' the place all the time."

Smith stood there looking at Jesse. He wasn't sure what to think. Was there someone else at the cabin, someone who was willing to help her? Smith continued to look at his foreman. Suddenly, the expression on his face changed as his eyes narrowed and he looked angry.

"You don't have the stomach for this, do you?" Smith asked.

"That ain't true, and you know it. I think she has some help, and I'm in no hurry to ride into a trap. Look at it this way. If we go after her thinkin' she has help and she does, then we will be prepared and won't be surprised. If she don't have help, then all the better. I'm not afraid, I just don't like surprises, especially surprises that can get me killed."

Again, Smith just looked at his foreman while he thought about what he had said. Maybe Jesse had something there, Smith thought.

"Excuse me, sir," one of the ranch hands said being very careful not to upset Smith.

"What it is, Bill?" Smith asked with anger in his voice at having his thoughts interrupted.

"Joe was sayin' that awhile back he shot and killed some man who looked like he was hunting for that narrow canyon that leads to the valley where that woman lives. Maybe, Bill didn't kill him like he said. Maybe he just wounded him and he got to the woman's cabin, and maybe she took care of him."

"Why wasn't I told about it before," Smith said.

"I don't know, sir."

Smith looked at the ranch hand for a moment. Maybe his ranch hand didn't kill the guy and he's at the cabin helping the woman. It was possible, Smith thought.

"Suppose I agree with you," Smith said, speaking to Jesse. "And we go after her thinking she has help, how does it make any difference? What do you suggest we do?"

"Well, from the looks of the sky there's a very good chance it'll start snowin' again almost any time now," Jesse said. "Snow will make it hard to follow her, plus it will be dark soon. I, for one, would not like to be tryin' to find my way to her ranch on the other side of that rocky ridge in the dark while it's snowin'. It's bad enough when it's dark without it snowin'. I think we should wait 'til mornin' and take a look at what the weather's like then. Then we can plan how we're goin' to handle it."

"Okay, but I want that valley ranch, and I don't care if I have to burn her out."

"If you think about it, the valley ranch won't be much good to yah 'til spring, anyway. That gives us time. In fact, it gives us all winter to get her out of there."

"You might be right, but I had better have that place by spring," Smith said harshly. "But she's not getting her horses or her cattle back, ever."

"Yes, sir," Jesse said, then turned and left for the bunkhouse.

Smith watched his foreman as he left the front porch, then turned and looked up the hill toward where the shots had come from and where Mrs. McDonald had yelled out her demand. While looking up the hill, he suddenly realized he still had the letter she had written in his hand. He looked at the letter for a moment. He was sure it was simply a repeat of what she had yelled at him about her livestock, but just to be sure, he turned and went inside the house. He sat down at his desk, opened the letter, and began reading it.

*Mr. Smith, I know you had my husband beaten to death, for that you will pay dearly. You will also pay for stealing my cattle and horses. The penalty for stealing cattle and horses, is hanging, and I plan to be there for your trial and for the hanging that will surely follow.*
*Mrs. McDonald*

Smith sat at his desk and stared at the letter. He had never had anyone stand up to him, much less threaten him or even challenge him, or try to stop him from getting anything he wanted. Now, all of a sudden, he had a woman not only challenging him, but threatening him as well. The fact that a mere woman would challenge him made his blood boil. He slammed his fist down on his desk and swore he would see to it that she was not in the cabin by spring.

The first thing that crossed his mind was he couldn't let her get away with it. He would have to stop her before word got out about what was going on. The fact that very few people even knew her husband was dead, and the only people that did were his ranch hands, made it seem possible for him to continue to go after her valley ranch.

In his mind, once people found out he had taken over the valley ranch, it would be easy to explain that her husband had died in an accident while cutting trees in the woods, and she had simply left and went to parts unknown. No one would miss her. That thought made him smile, and gave him a feeling of confidence that he would get the valley ranch by spring.

Smith took another look at the letter, stood up and walked over to the fireplace. He glanced at the letter one more time, then wadded it up and tossed it into the fire. He stood in front of the fireplace and watched the letter as it turned almost black before burst into flames. As soon as it had burned up, a smile came over his face.

"Your cabin will be the next thing that goes up in flames, then your barn," he said to himself. "Without your cabin and barn you will freeze to death."

Smith turned and looked out the window. He saw large wet snowflakes falling. He remembered what his foreman had said about it looking like it would snow again. Seeing the snow made him think about what else his foreman had said. Was he right that Mrs. McDonald had someone to help her, or was he just looking for an excuse not to go after her? The snow and the darkness of the night would make it very hard to find the trail over the ridge to her cabin, he admitted to himself.

Jesse Jones had been his foreman for a long time. He had been a loyal foreman and a good ranch hand through good and bad times. His judgment had been good most of the time in the past. Smith was beginning to think that maybe Jesse had been correct. He was certainly correct about the weather, and about the valley ranch being no use to him until spring. Maybe Jesse was right about Mrs. McDonald having someone to help her, too.

Smith was sure he had a lot to think about. With the change in the weather, there was nothing he could do tonight. He would get some sleep and talk to Jesse in the morning to plan how they were going to get Mrs. McDonald out of the valley.

Smith turned in, but sleep didn't come to him. The fact he had been shot at on his own porch kept his mind churning with anger. There was also the thought Jesse had instilled in his mind the idea that Mrs. McDonald might have someone there to help her defend the valley ranch.

How did she get the help? From what he had been told by his foreman and ranch hand, someone had almost gotten to the narrow canyon leading to her ranch. He knew how hard it was to find the valley. That thought led him to think whoever had come to her aid had to have had directions.

The next big question that came to his mind was how did she get the message out that her husband had been murdered? He began to think about it. As he thought about his men, he remembered who had been with him when he had Jacob McDonald beaten to death.

Like a sudden shock, he remembered one young cowboy who left the ranch the same day he had McDonald beaten. That was it. It had to have been the cowboy who was there when McDonald was beaten to death. That thought seemed to make sense to him.

It angered Smith a great deal to think the cowboy who had left had turned against him. Had he gone over to the other side to help protect Mrs. McDonald? Did she know he was with them when they attacked McDonald, or had he just gone there to help her without her knowing that he had worked for him?

Another thought came to mind. Did the young cowboy go into Custer City and talk to someone about what had happened? If so, who? If it had been the sheriff, the sheriff would have come right to Smith to question him. It probably wasn't the sheriff since the sheriff had not come out to his ranch.

It was the thought of the kid helping Mrs. McDonald that filled his thoughts. The more he thought about it, the more he didn't think the kid would help her. Smith doubted the young cowboy had the backbone to take him on.

Unable to come up with an answer of who was helping her, led him to think there probably wasn't anyone helping her. Since she had the guts to attack him on his front porch, she probably was ready for his ranch hands to go after her. She was most likely the one who shot at them as they ran up the hill after her. With that thought set in his mind, he found it much easier to clear his mind and fall asleep. The last thought that came to mind was to put a price on her head. He would pay the ranch hand who got her off the property, or killed her, five hundred dollars. He would tell them in the morning, but for now, Smith would get some sleep.

# CHAPTER TWELVE

As Susan lay beside Frank, she thought about what they had done. She wondered if they had accomplished anything, or if they had just made the situation worse. They had probably made Smith even more determined than ever to get the valley ranch away from her. The more she thought about it, the more concerned she became.

Smith was the kind of man who would not like it known that he had been attacked on his own property, especially by a woman. He would not like the embarrassment it would cause him if anyone outside the area ever got wind of what she had done and why she had done it. He would feel the need to get revenge and do it quickly.

But with all her thoughts about what Frank and she had done, the one thing that seemed to make sense to her was the fact they had done it together. For the first time, she was not alone in her battle to keep the valley ranch, even though the odds of keeping her valley ranch were still very slim. Lying next to her was someone who understood, someone who believed they could actually win a war against Smith.

As the hour grew late, a smile came across her face. She could feel the warmth of the man lying beside her. For the first time in months, she actually felt something other than hopelessness, something other than depression, and something other than loneliness. It was not something she could explain, not even to herself, but it felt real. Since she had never really been in love with anyone, she wasn't sure if what she was feeling was love for the man who laid beside her or if it was something else. Either way, it felt good.

She turned her head and looked at the man at her side. Although she had been a little embarrassed the first time she had been in bed with him, she no longer felt that way. They had taken the fight to Smith together. By doing that, it had brought them closer together.

"Are you okay?" Frank asked in a whisper.

The sound of his voice startled her. She didn't think he was awake. She wasn't sure how to answer him, or if she should, but he had been there for her. She decided she would answer him.

"Yes," she said softly.

"Are you sure?"

"Yes."

"What were you thinking about?"

Frank was hoping she would tell him. He had been lying in the bed thinking about the woman next to him. He wanted to know what she was thinking, but not sure he would like what she might say.

"I was thinking - - - well - - I was thinking about us," she finally said, instantly wishing she had not said anything.

"What about us?" he asked.

There was a long period of silence. Still not sure she should say anything more, she took a deep breath and let it out slowly. It took her a couple of minutes to build up her courage to say anything.

"I'm so glad you came here," she said softly, "but I think it was a foolish thing for you to do. You are risking your life to save my valley ranch when it really isn't much of a ranch."

Frank didn't know what to say. He thought about it for a little while before he said anything.

"Yes, I risked my life to come here, and I'm risking it to help you save your ranch; but I'm not sorry. You should not have to fight the likes of Smith without someone to stand by you, and help you, even if the odds of winning are small."

"I'm ready to die in my effort to keep my valley ranch out of Smith's hands because it means a lot to me. It is the only home I have ever had, and that I might ever have," she said with a hint of sadness in her voice.

"You are lucky. I have never had a place of my own to fight for. Maybe that is why I'm willing to help you fight for the place you call home. At least you can have something I wish I had, but will probably never have," Frank said with a sad note to his words.

She had heard the sadness in his voice, but didn't know what to say. She wondered what would become of her and the valley ranch if she won the war against Smith and lost the man beside her. That thought quickly brought a lot of mixed emotions running through her head.

Susan rolled over on her side so she was facing Frank. Even with just the glow of the fire in the fireplace, she could see he was looking at her.

"If we should somehow save the ranch from Smith, I would like you to call it 'home'," she said softly.

As soon as she said it, she could hardly believe what she had said. What would he think of her? Would he think she was being too forward? Did he think she was asking him to stay here and live with her? She wasn't sure he was the kind of man who would want to marry her, settle down and raise a few cattle, and maybe a family.

When it began to soak in what she had said, and the questions she had asked herself, she felt embarrassed. She quickly rolled over, turning away from him and moved as close to the edge of the bed as she could without falling out.

It was so quiet in the room all that could be heard were the faint sounds of the crackling of the fire as it warmed the small cabin. The longer the silence lasted the more the tension grew. All Susan could think about was what he must think of her. It was almost as if she had thrown herself at him, but she couldn't help herself. Lying next to her was the man she had taken in and cared for his wounds. In return, he had taken on her fight with Smith.

Frank laid there looking at the back of Susan's head. He wasn't sure what to think about her comment. Did she really mean it, or was it something she said out of a feeling of obligation for his help in fighting Smith? The longer he laid there looking at her, the more he wanted to let her know that he had been thinking about the valley ranch and how much he wished he had a place like it to call "home".

His thoughts turned to the woman lying in bed with her back to him. She had taken care of him, nursed him back to health, at least enough so he could help her. She had saved his life. He remembered the feel of her body when she held him against her. She was the most caring person he could ever remember meeting. Frank also understood she was lonely, having been left in the valley all alone. Frank couldn't help himself. He reached over and lightly put his hand on her shoulder.

"Susan," he said softly. "I would like very much to call your valley ranch my home."

He waited to see what her response would be to his comment. Frank would like to quit moving from place to place and have a place he could call home. A place where he could build something with someone, and maybe with the woman beside him. Susan was the kind of person he wanted to grow old with, caring, strong, loving, yet understanding.

Without a word, Susan turned over so she was once again facing him. She didn't say anything, rather she reached out and put her hand on his cheek. She felt his hand cover her hand. When he did that, she smiled. She wasn't sure if he could even see her face, but just touching her hand let her know he wanted to stay. All she needed to do was to make him feel welcome.

"I think it would be a good idea if we got some sleep." Frank suggested.

"I think you are right," she said reluctantly.

She removed her hand from his face and rolled over on her other side, all the time hopeful he would move closer to her and hold her in his arms. As she laid there in the darkness, she felt him move in the bed.

Frank was not sure it was a good idea, but he felt the urge, the need, to hold her close. He slipped his arm over her and tucked her close to him. He felt her tense a little, but she didn't resist. He could feel the warmth of her body through her night gown as he tucked her up against him. He wrapped his arm around her and held her tight. It was a feeling he had never known. Even though he had been with other women from time to time in his life, he had never felt more like he belonged in one place as much as he did at that moment.

It took Susan a little while to accept the feel of a man's body curled up behind her, but the feelings it gave her helped her to feel secure and safe. She wondered if it was going to last. Would Frank leave when it was over, or would he stay with her. Right now, it felt good to have him hold her, and that was enough to allow her to doze off into a restful sleep.

Susan woke early while it was still dark in the small cabin. She laid quietly when she discovered herself still wrapped in Frank's arms with one of his big hands gently cradling one of her breasts. Even though it surprised her a little, she liked the way it felt. It had been a long time since any man had touched her like Frank was. She listened in the quiet of the cabin. She could hear Frank breathing. It was clear he was still asleep. Without moving, she dozed off again, content in the comfort of his arms.

Sometime later, Susan woke from the feel of Frank's hand as he removed it from her breast then he carefully rolled away from her. She turned her head and looked over her shoulder at him as he sat up on the edge of the bed. There was an embarrassed look on his face, as if she had caught him doing something he wasn't supposed to do.

"Good morning," she said smiling at him.

"Good morning. How did you sleep?" he asked, almost afraid of what she would say.

"I slept very well. How about you?"

"I slept very well, too," he replied. "I'll get dressed and go take care of he horses."

"I'll get up and fix breakfast. We can eat when you come back in."

Frank just nodded, then stood up. He had his back to Susan as he dressed. As soon as he was finished, he turned and looked at Susan still lying in the bed. He smiled at her.

"I hope this doesn't upset you, but you are a very beautiful woman," Frank said.

He almost wished he hadn't said it when he saw it embarrassed her. He thought the best thing for him to do was to leave the cabin and take care of the horses, before he put more of his foot in his mouth than he already had. Frank turned and quickly left the cabin.

Susan laid in the bed and watched him as he left. His comment had embarrassed her, but she was glad he thought of her as beautiful.

She laid in the bed for a few minutes thinking of how good it felt to have a man hold her, especially Frank. Although he could be violent when it was called for, he had shown her that he could also be a gentle, loving man.

Suddenly, she realized she had better get out of bed and get dressed before he came back in and caught her with nothing on, and no breakfast on the table. She rolled out of bed and quickly dressed. She then stoked the fire and began fixing breakfast for the two of them.

All the time she was cooking, her thoughts were of Frank. If they survived their war with Smith, would he really want to stay there with her when it was over? Would he be happy living in the valley with her? When she thought about what happened during the night, she hoped he would like it there enough to stay.

Susan admonished herself for even thinking such a thing. Was the reason she was silently thinking he would want to stay and how much she wished he would because she had been so lonely? Was it because he was helping her fight against Smith to keep him from taking her valley ranch from her?

Those same questions had run through her mind before, but this time they seemed to be more important to her. She had to admit to herself that she wanted him to stay with her. With nothing to compare it to, she was sure that she was falling in love with him.

# CHAPTER THIRTEEN

Breakfast was almost ready when Frank returned to the cabin. He sat down at the table and watched Susan as she finished getting it ready and put it on the table. For a long time, nothing was said, the silence was heavy in the air. It wasn't until they were almost finished eating that either of them said anything. Susan was the first to speak.

"What's it like out there?"

"It's nice out. It warmed up a bit last night. Almost all the snow is gone. It must have stopped snowing shortly after we went to bed."

"We will have to keep our eyes open."

"Yes, we will. Susan, do you know if there are any caves or old mines in the area, especially on your property?" Frank asked.

Susan just looked at him. She had no idea what he was getting at, but she was sure he had a very good reason for asking.

"Not that I know of. Why do you ask?"

"I'm thinking it might be a good idea if we had another place to hide. It should be some place close where we could hold up for several days, even weeks, if necessary."

"I do remember in one of Jacob's letters to me, he said he lived here while he was building the cabin. The cabin was the first thing he built."

"Any idea where he stayed while he was building the cabin?"

"No," she said shaking her head."

"He must have had some sort of shelter. Maybe a tent or some other kind of shelter?"

"Not that I know of, but he could have had a shelter back in the woods. I wouldn't think it would be very far from here, because he said he worked on the cabin almost every day."

"I think it would be a good idea for me to go out and look around."

"But where would you start?"

"I think the best place to start would be behind the cabin just inside the woods. That would be the closest place where he might have had a shelter. There would be a lot of material he could use to build a small shelter to protect him from the weather when he would not be able to work on the cabin, and for a place to sleep."

"I'll go with you. With both of us looking, we might be able to find it faster." Susan said.

"I think it would be better if you to stay here and keep an eye on the place. If any of Smith's men should come around, fire a shot at them if you think you can hit them. If you can't, fire one shot to let me know they are around. I'll come as fast as I can."

Susan looked at him. There was no doubt in her mind he really meant what he said about shooting to hit any of Smith's men who might be nosing around on her property. Smith had threatened to take her ranch, and there was no doubt that he would take it by force, if necessary. It would not do any good to shoot to scare them away after what they had done to Smith.

"I mean it. If you get a chance to kill or injure one of Smith's men, do it. It is the only thing they understand," Frank said as he looked at Susan. "It is the only thing that will make them hesitate to attack you, and their hesitation gives us a small bit of an advantage."

"I know," Susan admitted reluctantly.

Frank got up, picked up his rifle from next to the door and turned to leave. He looked at Susan, then smiled.

Susan walked over to him and put her hands on his shoulders, then rose up on her tip-toes and kissed him lightly on the lips. He wrapped his free arm around her and held her to him as he looked down at her.

"Be careful out there," Susan said softly.

"I will. You be watchful from here. I'll never be very far away," Frank said then kissed her.

Reluctantly, Susan let go of him and watched him as he turned and left the cabin. As soon as he was outside and had closed the door, she went to the window to watch him as he disappeared around the corner of the cabin. Before letting the curtain fall back over the window, she looked around to see if she could see anyone sneaking around. She could not see anyone from the cabin.

As the time passed, she moved back and forth between the windows in the cabin, looking and watching for any sign of someone hanging around, or approaching the cabin or barn.

There were some areas she could not see from the cabin. She thought about going to the barn where she could see more of her valley ranch but decided against it. If anyone was snooping around behind the cabin, Frank would probably see them, she thought.

Meanwhile, Frank ducked into the woods directly behind the cabin. He hoped no one had seen him leave the cabin. He slowly began to move back into the woods far enough that he could still see the cabin, but deep enough that his movements might not be seen by anyone out in front of the cabin.

Frank began looking for some place where Jacob might have had a shelter of some kind. Moving slowly through the woods, he looked in all directions. He had gone about as far from the cabin as he thought he should without finding anything that might have been used for a shelter.

He moved a little deeper into the woods and headed back, walking parallel to where he had walked before. When he was directly behind the cabin, he stopped and looked around, but didn't see anything. Not seeing anything, he continued to search for some place where Jacob might have had a shelter.

He hadn't gone very far when he saw what looked like it could have been a shelter at one time. He carefully moved closer. As he approached it, he found there were a number of logs stacked in such a way that they hid the entrance to a cave. When he got up to it, he found that the logs had been stacked between the trees so they formed a log wall about six feet high and about six to eight inches thick. It even had a couple of well placed holes in it that would make good shooting ports. There were also several logs that ran from the top of the log wall to a rocky ledge just above and to either side of the opening to the cave.

Frank ducked down and looked in the cave and found it wasn't a cave, but a mine. Looking into it, he discovered it didn't go back very far which tended to make him think that Jacob had either found the mine, or he had dug it out to make it a temporary home while he built the cabin. The fact that it had a strong log wall in front made it much easier to defend, if needed.

It also gave Frank the impression that Jacob had built it in case he was attacked. It was like a small, very small fort. No matter the circumstances, Frank knew it was a place that could be used to continue the fight against Smith if he should manage to burn down the cabin and barn.

Frank started thinking about what supplies they would need to make it a place to fall back to should Smith drive them out of the cabin. As he was making a mental note of what they should put in the mine, he heard a gunshot. It sounded like it had come from in front of the cabin.

Frank started running toward the cabin when he heard a second shot, but it had come from the woods. Frank stopped and watched the area he thought the gunshot had come from before he moved. He spotted someone just inside the woods. He could see a man standing behind a tree with his gun pointed toward the cabin.

Frank quickly moved toward where the man was while using the trees to cover his advance toward the shooter. When he got to a position where he could see the man clearly, he stopped, raised his rifle and supported it in the notch of a tree. He took careful aim and pulled the trigger.

The sound of his rifle broke the moment of silence, and the man who was leaning against the tree ready to fire dropped to the ground with a thud. Frank had hit him square in the chest. Just as he was about to move, he heard the sound of a horse making tracks out of the area.

Frank saw a man on a horse riding away as fast as he could. He quickly fired a shot, but missed the rider. He took a second shot which hit the rider dumping him off the horse. The horse continued to run away. Frank looked toward the cabin, wondering if Susan was all right. He didn't dare go out in the open until he knew the area was clear of anyone else.

He worked his way to the first man he shot. He moved up to him carefully just in case he still had some fight left in him. When he got close to the man, he could see he was dead. He also could see the man's horse. It was tied to a tree several yards deeper in the woods.

Frank stepped up to the edge of the woods and waved his hat at the cabin. He could see the end of a rifle barrel sticking out the window. As soon as he started waving, the rifle barrel disappeared. He then stepped back into the woods and walked along the edge of the woods being very watchful to make sure there was no one else around.

When he got close to the man he had shot out of the saddle, he discovered he was still alive. Frank knelt down beside the man. The man looked up at him with fear in his eyes. Frank could see he had hit the man in the back, his bullet severing the man's spine as it passed through him. There was little doubt that the man would not live very long. The man coughed then quit breathing. Frank looked in the direction the man's horse had gone. There was little doubt the horse would return to the barn where it was from, that meant it would be going back to Smith's ranch.

Frank went back to where the first man had died, got his horse and put the man's body over the saddle. He then walked the horse deeper in the woods, well away from the cabin, where he pushed the body off the horse into a shallow ravine. He returned to the second man he had shot, put him over the horse and took him to the same spot than pushed the second man off the horse and into the ravine next to his partner.

After collecting the guns and ammunition he had taken from the men before dumping them in the ravine, Frank got in the saddle of the horse and rode the horse to the barn. He was removing the saddle from the horse when Susan came running into the barn.

"Are you all right?" she asked.

"I'm fine," Frank said as he turned to her.

"I was worried about you."

"It's all over for now, but I wouldn't take bets on when we get attacked again."

"I saw you shoot the one running away. Why didn't you just let him go?" she asked looking up at him.

"Two reasons. The first is he saw me. He would tell Smith that you have help. The last thing we want is for Smith to know you have help. It's one thing for him to think you have help, it's another for him to know it."

"Oh. I didn't think of that," she said feeling a little embarrassed.

"It's all right," Frank said. "The second reason is he won't be shooting at either of us again."

"Oh. What did you do with the two men?"

"I left them in a ravine deep in the woods for now. It would be my guess Smith will have his men come looking for them once the horse gets back home."

"Do you think he will come and get them," she asked.

"I seriously doubt he will. Smith doesn't care about the men who failed in their task. I plan to go out and bury them right where they are, but I didn't have a shovel. I'm also going to take their weapons and ammunition to a mine I found behind the cabin."

"A mine?" Susan asked, surprised. "Jacob never said anything about a mine?"

"I don't know why he didn't tell you about it, but it looks like it was his shelter while he built the cabin."

"Is it a gold mine?"

"I don't know if it was a mine, a cave or just a shelter he built among the trees and rocks. But the way he built it makes me think he expected to have trouble. He built it like a small fort."

"Will you show me where it is?"

"Of course. You may have to find it when I'm not here to help you. You can help me take the guns, ammunition and some supplies to the mine."

"What are you going to do with this horse?"

"Keep it for now."

Susan just looked at him as he turned and wiped down the horse with a rag. Once he was done, he gathered up the guns and ammunition the cowboys had and walked with Susan to the mine.

When they got to the mine, Susan stood outside the entrance to the mine and looked in.

"You might as well go in. It just might be our home if we can't stop Smith from destroying the cabin and barn, Frank said. "There's a lantern just inside on the left. You might want to light it.

Susan stepped into the mine, picked up the lantern and lit it. The light from the lantern gave her a chance to see the mine clearly. Although there was a fairly small entrance, one even she had to duck down to enter, it opened up into a fair sized room. It wasn't as big as the cabin, but two people could live reasonably comfortable in it, if necessary.

She noticed a small stove near the entrance with a stove pipe that would direct the smoke from a fire to the outside. There was a small bed, not really big enough for two but it could work if they snuggled up close. There was also a cabinet where she could store what she needed. After looking it over, she helped Frank carefully hide the guns and ammunition.

By the time they had the weapons in the mine and looked around a bit, it was a little past noon. Susan blew out the lantern then she returned to the cabin with Frank.

Frank took a horse and went into the woods to bury the bodies. It didn't take him long to bury the two men, he simply covered their bodies with dirt from the side of the ravine then covered the bodies with rocks from the bottom of the ravine. He rode the horse back to the barn and left it in a stall. Frank returned to the cabin and went inside.

"You look tired. Maybe you should lie down for awhile," Susan suggested.

"I think I will. My side is hurting from all the lifting."

Susan knew what he meant. Her first thought was she should have gone with him to help him bury the cowboys.

"Do you think you might have opened your wounds?"

"No. I just need to rest for a little while," he said then turned and walked over to the bed. He took off his boots and set them on the floor next to the bed, then took off his gun belt and hung it over a chair close to the bed. After he laid down, it wasn't long and he was sound asleep.

# CHAPTER FOURTEEN

While Frank laid resting, Susan busied herself sewing on a new dress so she wouldn't disturb him. A thought came to her as she sewed. If Smith wins their war with him, she would have little need for a new dress, but it kept her busy.

She looked over at Frank and wondered if they should continue the fight. She was risking his life by insisting on keeping the valley ranch. It would not be worth it if she won the battle and lost him. It also occurred to her that if she lost him, she would probably lose the valley ranch anyway, and probably her life.

Although she had never seen very much of Smith's ranch, she was sure he had a large number of men working for him. The question of how many of them would join in the fight came to mind. If it was but ten, the odds of winning the fight was still pretty slim.

The sudden sound of a rifle shot caused her to jump out of the chair and drop her sewing on the dirt floor. She ran to the window, drew back a corner of the curtain and looked outside.

It took Frank only a couple of seconds to be at her side. He picked up a rifle from next to the door and held it tightly in his hands as he watched Susan.

"What's going on out there?" Frank asked.

"There's a man on a horse. He has a white rag tied to the end of his rifle."

"How close is he?"

"He's too far for a shotgun to be of any use. He's just sitting out there looking toward the cabin."

"Is there anyone else around?"

Susan took a minute to look around, then turned to Frank.

"I don't see anyone else."

Frank looked across the room while thinking. He wondered if it was a trick to get her to open the front door and maybe step outside where she would be a target for someone nearby or for the man on the horse.

"Don't open the door," Frank said. "It might be a trick."

Frank was still thinking of what he should do when he noticed the shadow of a gun barrel on the curtains that hung over the side window. He raised his rifle and pointed it at the window. After judging where the sun was, he could quickly figure out where the man was standing. He put his rifle down and picked up a pistol and moved close to the window.

"Move away from the window," Frank said softly.

Susan quickly dropped the curtain and moved away from the window. As soon as she was clear of the front window, Frank raised the pistol close to the side window and cocked it. He then quickly pulled back the curtain with his free hand and fired the pistol. The man outside the window didn't have time to even duck. Frank's shot hit him right in the forehead and dropped the man right where he stood.

Frank quickly dropped the curtain, grabbed his rifle as he ran to the other window. He drew back the curtain and raised his rifle, but the man on horseback with the white rag was riding off as fast as his horse could carry him. Frank didn't have a good shot, so he let the man go without firing a single shot at him.

As soon as the man was out of sight, Frank turned and looked at Susan. She had her hands over her mouth and looked like she was in shock. Frank went to her and took her in his arms.

Susan laid her head on his shoulder as she tried to catch her breath. She was shaking all over with the realization they were trying to kill her. It took a couple of minutes before she was able to lean back a little and look up at Frank's face.

"What are we going to do?" Susan said with tears in her eyes. "They'll keep coming until they kill us."

"I think it's time to change our tactics. It's time to let Smith know we are not leaving."

Susan looked up at him as if he had gone crazy, then laid her head down on his chest and let him hold her. She wondered what more they could do to let Smith know that they were not going to leave.

"I don't think he will return or send out any more of his men today. We have shown him that he is going to have to come and get us himself, and he will have to do it with a larger force. We have proven he can't get this place with a few of his ranch hands taking shots at us."

"Are you sure?" she said as she lifted her head from his chest.

"Yes, I'm sure. He probably offered money to the man who kills you, sort of a bounty. That is why we are seeing them come at us two at a time."

"Is this place worth losing our lives over?" Susan asked as she looked up at him.

Frank looked down at her. After all they had been through, was she really ready to give it up, he wondered. It angered him a bit to think she was ready to give up and leave the valley ranch to Smith after all they had done to show Smith they were not leaving. He grabbed her shoulders and pushed her back so he could look down and see her face.

"You said I could make this valley ranch my home. Actually, you said I could call it my home. Did you mean that?"

"Yes," she replied softly while looking up at him as tears ran down her cheeks.

"Well, I'm not giving up the only place I can call home to the likes of Smith," he said with a hint of anger in his voice. "I will fight him to my last breath."

Susan looked at him. She could see in his eyes that he meant every word he said.

"I'm sorry. I guess I'm scared of what will happen to us," she said softly.

Frank continued to look at her face, then drew her close to him again. He held her tight and wished he had not been so harsh in what he said to her. She was scared and had every right to be.

"I'm sorry, too. I really want a place to call home more than just about anything. Can you understand that?"

"Yes. Yes, I can," she sobbed.

"This is already the place you call home. I want it to be my home, too," he said. "I'm willing to fight for it. Are you?"

Susan leaned back, straightened her shoulders and looked him right in the eyes. She knew she would have to be strong if they were going to keep their valley ranch out of the hands of Smith.

"Yes," she said softly, but with a hint of determination. "I'm ready to fight with you to keep our ranch."

"Then we best be getting ready."

Susan smiled up at him, then rose up on her tiptoes and kissed him. As soon as their lips met, she felt him pull her up against him, pressing her body tightly against his.

After a long kiss, Frank drew back a little and looked down at her. She looked up at him and smiled.

"We best get ready for a fight," she said.

"I have an idea."

"What's on your mind?"

"I think it will be awhile before Smith attacks us again. Sending a couple of men at a time to get you out has not been working for him. He will probably take a little time to form a plan. We need to take advantage of the time we have."

"Smith is a hothead. Do you really think he will take time to plan an attack?"

"Yes, I do. He has already lost several men. I seriously doubt he wants to lose more without getting the results he wants. The next time he comes at us he will come in force."

Susan took a moment to think about what he was saying. It seemed to make sense.

"I guess you're right."

"There's something else," Frank said.

"What's that?"

"I would be willing to bet Smith is getting worried about his men. If he keeps sending them out here, and they don't return; he might be getting worried the men still at his ranch will simply desert him or refuse to fight for him. But more importantly, he might be afraid that if any of them desert they might tell someone what is going on out here."

"You think word might get out about what is going on here?" she asked hopefully.

"It might, but I wouldn't count on it. Those who desert him aren't likely to admit that they had been attacking a widow to get her ranch away from her, even if it was for their boss. They are more likely to head off to somewhere where they are not known and keep quiet about it."

"What do we do now? What was your idea?" Susan asked.

"Oh. I was thinking it just might be a good time to let Smith know we are mad as hell at him," Frank said.

"And just how do you plan on doing that? Don't you think he already knows that we are mad as hell at him?"

"I'm sure he thinks we are, but I plan to make sure he knows it. I plan to make sure he knows just how mad we are," Frank said with a grin.

"Okay, what's your plan?"

"I plan to attack him again."

Susan just looked at him. There was little doubt in her mind that he meant what he said.

"Okay. I'm ready for anything."

Frank was glad to hear she was ready to help him.

"The first thing we have to do is get supplies to the mine, just in case we need to retreat to it. There's even room to put a couple of horses under cover at the mine."

"Are we moving to the mine?"

"Not really. We are just supplying the mine with things we will need if we should lose the cabin and barn."

"If we lose the cabin and barn, will we not lose the ranch?" Susan asked.

"We will only lose the buildings. We can rebuild the cabin and barn. If we lose them, we will have the mine to fall back on," Frank said reassuringly. "Before Smith finds out, let's get things together and stock the mine as if we are going to live there."

Susan gave Frank another kiss, then began gathering cooking pots and pans as well as some of the basic food stuffs that would be easy to store. Frank gathered some feed and put it on the backs of two of the horses they had obtained from those who had attacked them.

After packing up as much as the horses could carry, they led the horses back into the woods to the mine. He watched for anyone who might be around, but saw no one. Walking the horses under the shelter in front of the mine, he tied them to a post and removed the supplies.

Susan went into the mine and started to put things away as if they were going to be living there. She had just finished putting the few pots and pans in the cabinet when Frank entered. She turned and looked at him.

"It's smaller than the cabin, but it will do if we have to use it for the winter," she said.

"I'm hoping that we don't have to use it all winter, but if we have to, it will do," Frank agreed.

Frank and Susan continued to get the mine set up as a place to live, but hoping it would not be necessary. Frank closed in the sides between the mine and the log wall with the overhanging tarp so it could be used to keep the horses out of sight. He left a small opening on each side for a place to escape from it, if necessary.

Once they had finished getting the mine ready, they returned to the cabin. They settled in for the rest of the day. While Susan prepared a meal, Frank spent most of his time moving from one window to the other, keeping an eye out for danger.

When it got dark, they decided it would be a good idea if they kept watch during the night in order to keep from being surprised if Smith should have his men attack them at night. Frank agreed to take the first watch.

Susan got ready for bed while Frank kept watch. Once she was ready, she walked over to Frank and kissed him, then climbed into bed.

"Wake me if you get tired," Susan said.

"I will. Get some sleep."

It was very quiet once Susan was in bed. Frank had blown out the lantern. The only light in the cabin was the soft glow of the fireplace. As time passed, Frank quietly moved back and forth from one window to the other while keeping an eye out for danger.

# CHAPTER FIVETEEN

Smith was standing on the porch of his ranch house when one of his ranch hands came riding toward the ranch house as if his tail was on fire. He pulled up in front of the ranch house and jumped down from his horse then stepped up on the porch. The ranch hand was out of breath, and the expression on his face showed he was scared.

"Well, did you get her?" Smith asked with a harsh tone to his voice.

"No, sir," the ranch hand said as he tried to catch his breath. "We didn't, sir."

"What happened?" Smith demanded.

"I rode up to the front of the cabin, like we planned," he said then paused for a moment to take a couple of deep breaths while trying to get his thoughts together.

"I stayed back far 'nough from the cabin so she couldn't use that shotgun on me. Will, he worked his way 'round the barn and up 'longside the cabin. I had a white cloth tied on the end of my rifle so she wouldn't shoot at me," he said then stopped to take another deep breath.

"Get to it, man," Smith said angrily.

"Well' sir, as soon as Will let me know he was ready, I fired a shot in the air to get the woman's attention out in front of the cabin. Like we planned. I seen the curtain in the front window move so I knew she was lookin' out the window. She suddenly closed that curtain, and in a couple of seconds, there was a shot fired out the side window, the one facin' the barn, and I seen Will drop to the ground with a hole in his head," the ranch hand explained excitedly. "I don't know how she knew he was there, but she shot him dead. I swung my horse around and got the hell out of there."

"Did you see anyone else around?" Smith asked, obviously angry that they had failed to get her.

"No, sir. That young woman is tougher than any woman I've ever met. It's almost as if she knew Will was there."

"Did you see any signs of Ray or Roth, or the horse Ray was riding? The horse Roth was riding came back without him."

"No, sir. I didn't see anythin' of 'um. Once I seen Will get shot, I hightailed it out of there."

"Go tell Jesse I want to talk to him, NOW!" Smith demanded.

"Yes, sir," the ranch hand said.

The ranch hand jumped off the porch of the ranch house and ran toward the bunkhouse to get Jesse. It wasn't long before Jesse came running toward the ranch house. He jumped up on the porch and looked at Smith.

"What's up, boss? Juan looked like he'd seen a ghost," Jesse said.

"It's about time we take matters into our own hands. Offering a reward for getting that woman out of the valley has proven to do nothing to get her out of there. Six men have tried to collect my reward and all of them have failed. Five of them have not come back," he said with a tone of anger in his voice.

Jesse knew of only four that had taken the challenge to get her out of the valley, and only one of them returned. He knew about two others who had decided that they didn't want any part of killing a woman and had left for the Wyoming Territory, but Jesse wasn't about to say anything about them to Mr. Smith.

The two that left for Wyoming Territory knew that it would not be wise for them to say anything about why they left good paying jobs. It was their intent to just disappear and never say a word about what was going on at the valley ranch for fear they would be hung for not trying to stop the attacks on Mrs. McDonald.

"What do you have in mind, boss?"

"Tomorrow morning we are going to find a way over the ridge and into the valley ranch where we can come up behind it. We are going to set fire to the cabin and the barn."

"How do you plan to do that? Every time anyone gets close to the cabin or barn, they end up dead. That woman is very good with a gun," Jesse said.

"I thought about it a lot last night and I came up with a plan. We are going to do it in such a way that the blame will be put on someone else. We will sneak over there and shoot flaming arrows at the cabin and barn. If we get behind the barn, we might be able to get close enough to shoot flaming arrows through the loft door into the hay stacked in the barn. Once that starts burning, there will be no stopping it, and the barn will burn to the ground.

"While that woman is busy trying to save the barn, we'll set the cabin on fire in the same way. The best part is it will be blamed on the Indians," Smith said with a grin.

"That would certainly make her leave," Jesse said.

"I don't want her to just leave, I want her unable to tell anyone what happened."

Jesse looked at his boss. There was little doubt in his mind that his boss wanted her dead, so she couldn't tell anyone what happened. Jesse was thinking that at this point, it might be best if she was dead; so she couldn't tell anyone what was going on.

"I want ten men ready to ride before the sun comes up. You pick men that will have no problem with what I want them to do, you understand?" Smith asked, interrupting Jesse's thoughts.

"Yes, sir," Jesse said, then turned and went back to the bunkhouse.

Jesse picked out the men he knew would keep their mouths shut and had no qualms about killing or burning anything or anyone for a few extra bucks. He took them off to a room in the boss's house where they could talk without any of the other ranch hands being able to hear them, and where Jesse could explain what they were to do and how they were to do it. After he explained everything, he asked if there were any questions.

"What about the woman?" one of them asked.

"She is not to get out of there alive," Jesse said as he looked at the men.

"If she dies as a result of the fire that would settle it for the boss, wouldn't it?" another one asked.

"That would indeed settle it for the boss," Jesse replied.

"What do we get for this?"

"The money offered for the person to get rid of her still stands, but it will be split up among all of you. That amounts to two hundred and fifty dollars each."

"I'm in," one of them said with a wide grin.

It was immediately followed by the same response from the other nine men. Jesse had the men he needed to comply with Smith's order.

"Keep this among yourselves," Jesse reminded them. "The law doesn't take kindly to killin' a woman. If anyone of you talks, you can surely bet that all of us will hang."

"It don't go out of this room," one of them said as he looked around the room getting a quick agreement from the rest of them.

"If all goes well, it will look like Indians attacked the valley ranch, killed the woman and burned the buildings to the ground," Jesse said.

"There ain't been an attack by injuns for a good long time around here," one of the men protested.

"There's a small tribe of Indians who live just a little way from here," Jesse said.

"Well, it looks like they got upset about somethin'," one of them said with a laugh.

Several others laughed at his comment. As far as the men were concerned, it was a plan that should be easy to carry out, and would not leave any suspicion on them. Since the Indians would get blamed for it, the army would be looking for the Indians who had killed the woman and burned down her buildings.

With everything settled and the men picked for the job, Jesse sent them off to return to their usual work while he left the room and went to find Mr. Smith. He was told by the cook that Mr. Smith was in his room.

Jesse knocked on the door then waited for Mr. Smith to answer. He saw the look on Mr. Smith's face when the door opened. He wasn't sure what to think.

"Well?" was all Smith said.

"I have ten men ready and willin' to join you in getting the woman out of the valley."

"Good. Will they be ready first thing in the morning?"

"Yes, sir. I told them that there would be two hundred and fifty dollars over and above their usual pay for each of them when the job is done."

"Good. I guess we are ready," Smith said.

"You mentioned that we were going to use arrows to set fire to the barn and cabin. Where are we going to get arrows and the bows to shoot them?"

"You will find them in the large box in the locked room in the barn. I have had them for years. I knew they would come in handy one day," Smith said with a hint of a grin.

"May I ask where you got them?"

"From the Indians who tried to keep me from building my ranch here," he said with a grin. "I raided their camp one night and killed every one of them; then took all their weapons, including their knives, bows, arrows, rifles, everything."

Jesse didn't say anything more. He knew that Smith was a ruthless man, but he never realized just how ruthless. He remembered hearing about the slaughter of a small group of Indians a number of years ago, but it was thought that it had been carried out by another tribe of Indians because all their weapons had been taken along with blankets and other items that Indians would use.

"I want the men you picked ready to ride at sunup."

"Yes, sir. They will be ready," Jesse said, then turned and left the ranch house.

Smith followed Jesse to the front door and watched him leave. He was feeling pretty good about his plan. With all that had happened so far, he was more than willing to kill Mrs. McDonald to get the valley ranch. The more he thought about it, the more he wanted her dead. Not just to keep her from talking, but to get his revenge for attacking him on his front porch and shooting at him.

Alive, she could still cause him problems. It would be her word against his, but someone just might believe her and start looking into what really happened in the valley.

Smith turned and went back into the ranch house. He began to pace up and down in front of the fireplace. His thoughts turned to the men he was missing. It passed through his mind that one or two of them might have simply left the area. It concerned him, but not so much as to make him stop his attack on Mrs. McDonald. All it did was make him want to get control of the valley ranch as quickly as possible.

It was getting late when Smith turned in for the night. He didn't sleep very well. His mind was filled with the excitement of finally getting the valley ranch and getting rid of that damn wisp of a girl from a big city back east. He was still irritated by the demands she had made of him. All though he admired her fortitude, he didn't admire it so much

that he would let her keep her valley ranch.  He would have
the valley ranch by tomorrow.

# CHAPTER SIXTEEN

It was still dark when Susan woke. The only light in the small cabin was from the glow of the fire in the fireplace. She looked toward the window and saw Frank standing next to it looking out. She wondered what he was thinking.

"Is everything all right?" she asked.

He turned and looked at her before he spoke, "I think we should take everything you need to the mine before it gets light.

Susan quickly sat up on the edge of the bed.

"What's wrong?" she asked.

"I have a feeling there could be trouble this morning, or at least before the day is done." His voice showed he was worried.

"I'll get dressed," she said as she stood up.

It didn't take her but a few minutes to get dressed in men's trousers and shirt. She didn't worry about Frank seeing her getting dressed, she didn't even think about it. From the sound of Frank's voice there was no time to waste. As soon as she was ready, she went to him. He was still standing at the window.

"Do you see something?"

"No, but the rider that got away yesterday will tell Smith what happened here."

"Do you think he knows that I didn't shoot the man next to the cabin?"

"I doubt it, but it would be the thing that would make Smith mad as hell. A man with his temper will probably want to seek revenge and do it quickly."

"What do you want me to do?"

"Gather up as much food as you can. I'll get our horses out of the barn and take them to the mine. Since there is only room for two horse at the mine, I'll take the two horses at the mine now to the small patch of grass I saw well back of the mine. I'll hobble them there for now."

Frank left the cabin for the barn. He saddled both horses, then took them to the mine. He took the saddles off the horses, stored them in a corner inside the mine. He then took the two horses he got from the men he had killed to a patch of grass in a small clearing behind the mine. He hobbled them in the clearing. It was far enough away from the mine and deep enough in the woods where Smith or any of his men were not likely to find them. Keeping Susan's and his horse under the cover at the mine would assure him that they would not be seen. He then returned to the cabin.

As he walked into the cabin, he noticed Susan was standing there looking around the cabin as if there was something she forgot. She looked sad. He wondered if she was thinking that it might be the last time that she would see her cabin. There was little doubt in Frank's mind that she might be right.

As Frank looked around the cabin, he noticed she had piled most of the food on the table. He also noticed that a bible was also on the table.

"We better get moving. It will be light soon. I would hate to have Smith or any of his men catch us away from any kind of protection."

"I'm sure you're right. I just hate the thought that this cabin and barn might be destroyed."

"I understand," Frank said as he moved close to her and put his arms around her. "If it is destroyed, we will just have to build a new cabin and barn. And we'll do it together."

She looked up at him and said softly, "I would like that."

Frank leaned down and kissed her. It was not a long kiss, but one that told her he loved her and planned to stay here and rebuild if necessary.

"We need to get moving," Frank said.

They worked together to gather the rest of the food onto a blanket, then wrapped it up. Frank took the blanket and put it over his shoulders and started out the door. Susan followed him with her bible and her quilt in her arms along with the rest of the food. They carried their supplies to the mine and set them down inside.

"Susan, do you see that opening in the logs in front of the mine?" Frank asked as he pointed to the logs.

"Yes."

"I want you to take a rifle and go over there to keep a watch for anyone coming this way. If you see someone, don't shoot unless he might find you, but be ready to shoot. Do you understand?"

"Yes," she said looking up at him. "I'm to shoot to kill."

"That's right, because they will be coming to kill you. Things have gone too far. At this point they can't afford to let you live. If anyone finds out what has been going on here and the law catches up to them, they will probably be hung. That is enough to make them want you dead."

"I understand, but where are you going?"

"I'm going to that outcropping of rocks up behind the barn where I can see what is going on. Keep a watch for me, too. I may have to retreat back this way in a hurry."

"I'll watch for you," she assured him.

"It will be light soon. I better get into position," he said as he leaned down and kissed her.

After kissing her, he quickly turned and ran off into the woods. It wasn't long before he disappeared from Susan's sight. As soon as he was out of sight, she took a rifle and a box of ammunition and went to the opening in the logs. She set the ammunition on one of the logs then made sure the rifle was ready to use before she looked out through the opening. The opening gave her a fairly wide field of view, but she could not see the cabin or barn from the mine because of the trees.

Frank hurried to the rocky outcropping that overlooked the barn and cabin. He came up behind it so that no one would see him. He found a place where he could see the back of the barn and part of the back of the cabin. He settled in among the large rocks and just waited and watched. It was a good vantage point to see who might come over the ridge.

He hadn't been there very long when he heard something moving in the woods off to the left of his position. He quickly swung himself around, keeping low and behind the large rocks. He pointed his rifle in the direction of the sounds. It wasn't long and he could hear voices.

"It's over that way," one of the voices said.

Frank finally got sight of who was moving through the woods. He only recognized one of them, but it was enough for him to know who they were. The one he recognized was Smith, and he had eleven other men with him, probably some of his ranch hands.

"Okay," Smith said. "Keep quiet and move carefully. I don't see anyone around, but that doesn't mean she is not being watchful. You guys with the bows, you move in as close as you can and fire your arrows into the barn through the windows and the loft door."

Frank watched as five of the men moved ahead of the others. He could see them move toward the end of the barn. It didn't take him but a second to figure out what they were planning to do. They were going to set the barn on fire. He took careful aim at Smith.

"Damn," he said to himself.

From his position in the rocks, he would not have a clean shot at Smith. Smith was very hard to see through the trees. He knew that if his bullet should strike a branch or even a twig on its way to its target, there was a good chance it would miss him. Frank couldn't afford to miss Smith with so many of his men around.

He hated to just lie there among the rocks and watch as Smith's men lit the arrows and shot them into the barn, but there was nothing he could do without giving away his position. He certainly could not take on all of Smith's men by himself.

As soon as the barn was burning and the fire could be seen through the windows in the barn, Smith started to move in a little closer to the cabin.

"Keep an eye on the cabin. Shoot anyone who tries to get out. You two move around so you can see the front door. Don't let her escape."

Frank not only watched as they torched the cabin, but he heard Smith's order to kill Susan if she tried to escape the fire. From what Smith had said, Frank was sure he didn't know that Susan had help. He wanted so much to kill Smith, but it would not be a good idea, at least not now. If he tried, there would be eleven men to deal with, not the best odds. He couldn't afford to get himself shot and leave Susan alone to face Smith's men. They couldn't afford to let her live. They had already gone too far.

For the time being, all Frank could do was to let the cabin and barn burn to the ground. The one thing he was sure of was that Smith was going to pay for it, and pay dearly.

Frank sat there and watched. He was fuming mad, and vowed that he would make Smith pay for what he had done, but for now he had someone else to worry about, Susan.

It was a new feeling for Frank. He had never had anyone else to worry about before. It was the first time in his life he had someone who needed him, and whom he needed. He was no longer alone in the battle with Smith as he had been in battles he had had in the past.

As the cabin became totally engulfed in flames, he could see the men move in closer to the buildings. The roof of the barn fell in first, followed closely by the cabin's roof. The men gathered around the burning buildings as Smith rode up close to check out their handy work.

"Did anyone see her come out of the cabin or barn?" he asked.

"I think we must have caught her sleepin'. The cabin went up pretty fast. She must have died in the cabin," Jesse said.

"Are you sure?" Smith asked.

"No one saw her get out of the barn or the cabin," Jesse reassured Smith.

"There's no way she could have survived that fire," one of the ranch hands said.

Smith got off his horse and stood in front of the cabin and watched the fire slowly consume it and everything in it. He continued to watch it until it was just a pile of burning rubble. When he looked up from the fire, he could see his men standing around the remains of the two buildings. As Smith continued to look around, he began to realize that no one could have gotten out of either of the two buildings alive, and a grin started to come over his face.

Smith turned his back to the fire and looked over the valley. The valley was all his now, he thought to himself. The buildings in the valley were not important to him. He wanted the valley to pasture his cattle during the long hot summers.

His thoughts were interrupted by Jesse walking up beside him. Smith turned and looked at his foreman.

"I think we are done here," Jesse said.

"No, we are not," Smith said. "I want everything possible done to remove any sign that anyone had ever lived here."

Jesse looked at his boss as if he didn't know what he was saying.

"I want the chimney torn down and the rocks scattered. I want anything left that even hints that someone might have settled here gone. Any pots or pans, anything that didn't get burned up in the fire, I want removed and buried."

"There's a hell of big spot on the ground that was burned. What do we do about that?"

"That will be taken care of by next spring when the grass grows over it. I want it to look like it was burned by a lightning strike."

"Yes, sir," Jesse said thoughtfully. "But what about those who knew that McDonald had lived here, and knew he had a cabin and a barn?"

Smith looked at Jesse and thought a moment about what he had said before he spoke.

"You have a point. Make it look like the Indians burned it down by leaving the chimney. Come spring we will let the sheriff know that the McDonald ranch had apparently been attacked by Indians and the place had been burned to the ground.

"Yes, sir," Jesse said.

"You've got your orders. I'm returning to the ranch. I'll leave you with five men to make sure there is nothing left but the fireplace. It has to look like it was caused by Indians burning it down."

"Yes, sir," Jesse said as he watched his boss get back in the saddle.

Jesse turned and looked at the smoldering pile of rubble. He knew it was going to take the better part of the day for the fire to burn out. He glanced up in time to see his boss and five of the ranch hands ride off into the woods.

Frank sat in among the rocks at the rocky outcropping above and behind the barn. He watched what was going on. He saw Smith and several of his men ride off leaving six men behind. He wondered why he had left the men.

It wasn't until the fire and been reduced to mostly coals that the six remaining men began to move around. Five of the men mounted their horses and began riding around the smoldering remains of the cabin and barn. Frank was certain that they were making sure there was nothing left that would indicate anyone other than the Indians had been responsible for setting the buildings on fire.

Frank could see the sixth man looking around at the still smoldering remains of the cabin. The man then walked around what was left of the barn, which was a pile of smoldering logs and hay.

After the man had looked over the remains of the barn and cabin, he walked over to his horse. He got back in the saddle and left the valley the same way they had come into it, with the other five men following.

As soon as they had left and Frank could no longer see them, he left his place of hiding and returned to the mine. When he arrived at the mine, he was greeted by Susan.

"I saw a lot of smoke. Do we still have a barn and cabin?" she asked thinking she already knew the answer.

"I'm afraid they burned them both to the ground."

The look on Susan's face showed that she was not surprised, but was very disappointed.

"I guess we will just have to build a new cabin and barn," she said softly, trying to be as positive about it as she could, but not doing very well at it.

"I guess we will, but it's not over. They think that you died in the fire. Once they find out you are alive, they will be coming at us with all they have," Frank said. "Smith would not like it if you got away and were able to tell the sheriff about what he and his men did here in his efforts to get you out of this valley."

"I know," she said with a sigh of disappointment. "What's our next move?"

"Our next move is to get a good night's rest and decide what we are going to do tomorrow."

"I have a suggestion," she said looking up at him.

"What's that?"

"I think we should get something to eat before we get that good night's rest. We haven't eaten all day."

"That does sound like a good idea. I'll keep watch while you fix us something to eat."

"Okay," Susan said then turned and went into the mine to make dinner.

Frank turned and stood at the log wall in front of the mine. He was thinking about what they should do next. They could leave and tell the sheriff what was going on, but where was the proof. The sheriff would certainly want proof before he would take any kind of action against someone like Smith. Smith was a pretty powerful man in the county. The only proof they had was the remains of the burned cabin and barn, but the sheriff might think they burned down as the result of an accidental fire, or because some renegade Indians attacked them and set the cabin and barn on fire. Smith would also have the word of his ranch hands who were going to side with him, if for no other reason than to save their own skin.

The more Frank thought about what had happened and their chances of getting the sheriff to investigate, the more he realized they were going to have to take care of themselves. With that thought in mind, he started to think of ways to protect the valley from Smith taking it over.

He was just starting to think of a plan to let Smith know he had not won, and that the war was not over, when Susan stepped outside the mine. She walked up to him and took him by the arm.

"Dinner's ready," she said as she walked with him into the mine. "Do we need to keep a watch while we eat?"

"No, I don't think we need to keep a watch for at least a couple of days. Smith will not want to move his cattle up here until spring. As far as he is concerned, you are dead and I don't exist. That should give us sometime to decide what we are going to do."

Susan and Frank went into the mine and sat down to eat. It was obvious they were hungry by the way they ate. Nothing was said until they were almost finished.

"What do we do now?" Susan asked as she looked into Frank's eyes.

"I'm not sure; but whatever it is, it will have to be done by us."

"It might be a good idea if we get some rest."

"I agree with that. It has been a long day."

"The only thing we have to do is to keep our eyes and ears open anytime we leave here. I have no idea if anyone might come by to check and make sure the fire is out. And if it snows, we will have to be very careful not to leave any tracks in the snow that might be seen by someone just nosing around."

"I'm not going anywhere tonight. I'm going to get ready for bed," Susan said.

"Sounds like a good idea."

Susan moved over next to the bed and took off her clothes. She slipped into a night gown then laid down on the bed. She laid as close to the edge of the bed as possible leaving just enough room for Frank.

Frank blew out the lantern, got ready for bed then slipped under the covers. He no more than laid his head down when Susan rolled up against him. He tucked her in close, letting her rest her head on his shoulder and her arm across his chest. It had been a long and stressful day and they were both tired. It wasn't long before they were asleep.

# CHAPTER SEVENTEEN

When morning dawned Susan and Frank were still curled up together. Susan was wrapped in Frank's arms. She felt his breath against the back of her neck, and his hand lying gently against one of her breasts. She felt she was safe and secure with him holding her. Even with all that had happened over the past months, she was convinced that everything would work out. She had no idea why she felt that way since Smith was still around, the cabin and barn had been burned to the ground, and they were hiding out in an old mine.

Suddenly she felt Frank move. He took his hand off her breast and rolled over on his back. He turned his head and looked toward Susan only to find her looking over her shoulder at him.

"Good morning," she said with a smile.

"Good morning. Are you ready to get up?"

"Not really," she replied as she turned toward him.

"I'll get up and let you sleep some more."

"I would prefer you give me a morning kiss."

Frank looked at her, then slowly rolled toward her. He leaned down over her until their lips met. It wasn't a very passionate kiss, but it was one that said they were growing close.

Their moment of closeness was interrupted by the sound of a horse. Frank let go of her, quickly rolled out of bed, grabbed a rifle then quickly moved toward the opening of the mine. He pushed back the tarp that covered the opening and looked out. The two horses that he had kept close were looking off to the left of the mine.

Frank stepped out of the mine and moved close to the tarp that hung between the rock wall of the mine and the log wall in front. He slowly pulled back the tarp and looked out. He didn't see anything for a moment or two.

Only after carefully searching the area, he saw a horse standing about fifty yards from the mine. It wasn't until the horse moved that he saw an Indian on the horse's back. It wasn't until the Indian moved slowly toward where the cabin had been that Frank noticed the Indian had two horses in tow. He quickly recognized the horses as the ones he had taken from the two men he had killed, and that he had left grazing in a small clearing back in the woods behind the mine.

"We've got company," Frank said softly to Susan. "Get my pants and coat."

It didn't take Susan but a moment to get his pants and coat. She took them out to him, then watched the Indian while Frank got dressed.

"He's taking the horses," she said, as the Indian moved slowly through the woods toward where the cabin and barn had been.

"Yeah, but I think there's more to it. It would be my guess that he saw the smoke from the fires and stumbled on the horses when he came to investigate," Frank said as he finished dressing.

"What are you going to do?"

"I'm going to talk to him, I hope," he said then turned and looked at her. "Get dressed."

Susan looked at Frank. He winked at her, then quickly moved out of the shelter and ducked behind a large tree.

Since the Indian was walking the horses slowly through the woods, Frank was able to silently get close to the Indian. When he was only about fifteen feet directly behind the Indian, he let the Indian know he was there.

"Don't move," Frank called out.

The Indian stopped the horses, then very slowly turned his head and looked over his shoulder at Frank. He instantly knew that there was no chance for him to defend himself, or to run as Frank had his rifle pointed at him.

"Do you speak English?" Frank asked, still keeping his gun on the Indian.

"Yes, but not good," the Indian said.

"Where do you think you are going with my horses?"

"I found 'um back there," he said as he pointed in the general direction of where Frank had left them.

"My name is Frank. What is your name?"

"My name is Red Owl. I am a Sioux."

"What are you doing here, Red Owl?"

"I saw smoke. I come to see where it come from."

"Are you alone?"

"Yes. I want no trouble. You say they are your horses, then I will leave them with you."

"I don't want any trouble, either," Frank said as he lowered his rifle, stepped up close to the Indian and took the reins of the two horses.

"I will let you go on your way. The smoke is from the cabin and barn in the valley. They were set on fire by some white men in such a way as to make it look like Indians set fire to them."

"I didn't think any of my people would set them on fire. I do not want my people blamed for it."

"We do not blame you. We know who set them on fire."

"I'll go back to my people and tell them what happened here. They will be glad to know that white men burned the cabin and barn."

"Return to your people safely."

The Indian nodded his head then turned his horse around and headed back the way he had come. Frank stood and watched the Indian as he rode away. As soon as the Indian was out of sight, Frank returned to the mine, tying the horses just outside the tarp covered entrance.

"I see that the Indian has turned and gone back. What was he doing around here?" Susan asked.

"He saw the smoke and came to see what happened. He just stumbled on the horses."

"Where is he going?"

"Back to his people to tell them about the smoke and that white men started the fire."

"What do we do now?"

"I think we should have breakfast, then plan our next move," Frank said as he moved close to her.

Susan went into the mine and started making breakfast while Frank took care of the horses. It wasn't long before breakfast was ready and she had called Frank in to eat.

As he sat down at the small table to eat, he looked at Susan. He thought about her and wondered how much more of their fight with Smith she would able to stand. There was little doubt that they would be spending most of the winter in the mine even if they won their little war against Smith.

"What's on your mind? You have hardly touched your breakfast."

"I'm sorry. I was thinking."

"About what?" she asked as she looked at him for some idea of what was on his mind.

"I was thinking about us."

"What about us?" she asked.

"It could be a very long winter, and we would have to spend it here in this small mine; sometimes not being able to leave for days on end," he said then stopped talking.

"What are you saying? Don't you think we can get along if we are stuck in this mine together?"

"No, I'm not saying that. What I'm getting at is there is nothing to do if we get snowed in. We could get on each other's nerves."

"I guess we would have to find something to keep us busy," she said with a smile.

Frank couldn't help but like the fact that she was smiling. He quickly returned to eating the breakfast Susan had made for them. As he ate he began to think about Smith.

"I've got an idea," Frank said, but he wasn't sure how she would feel about it.

"What's your idea?"

"We now have enough horses to get out of here."

"I will not leave my valley ranch," she insisted.

"Wait. Hear me out."

"Okay," she said while looking at him.

"McDonald had registered this valley with the county land registry, right?"

"Yes, of course. That was what made Smith so mad. Jacob had filed on it before Smith thought to do it," Susan said wondering what Frank was getting at.

"Smith cannot take possession of the property until he can show that both you and your husband are dead, or that you have abandoned the property. Right?"

"True," she said as she began to understand what he was getting at.

"This is what I want you to do. We have a couple of extra horses. I want you to take them and go to Four Mile Stage Stop. From there you will go to Custer City and visit with the sheriff. You will tell him what is going on out here."

"I will not leave my valley ranch," she said sharply.

"I understand how you feel about this ranch, but so do I. The reason I want you to go is the fact that it is your valley ranch. You are the one who must file a complaint against Smith."

"But you know the sheriff. He would believe you. Besides, it was one of Smith's men that shot you," she argued.

"I can't prove it was one of Smith's men. I never saw who shot me. Now, you could get the sheriff to believe you when you file a complaint of murder against Smith."

"What if Smith sees me? He will know that I wasn't killed in the fire."

"I'm going to leave for awhile. I'm going to find that Indian who was here this morning and see if he will take you to Four Mile Stage Stop. I'm sure he would know a way around Smith's property so Smith would not see you," Frank said. "Think about it while I go find that Indian."

"Are you sure it is safe for me to travel with him?" Susan asked with a look of concern.

"Yes," Frank said then left the mine and saddled a horse.

Susan watched as Frank rode off into the woods. It wasn't very long before he was out of sight.

Frank rode as fast as he could, following the tracks left by the Indian's horse. Although the Indian had ridden his horse at a walk, he had still covered a lot of ground. As soon as Frank saw the Indian through the trees, he called to him.

"Red Owl, wait."

The Indian stopped and looked over his shoulder to see who it was calling to him. He quickly recognized Frank. He waited for Frank to ride up beside him.

"Why do you come after me?" Red Owl asked.

"I need your help. In return for your help, I will give you the two horses you returned to me this morning."

"It must be important if you will give me two horses."

"It is. I need you to take my woman to the Four Mile Stage Stop. I need you to make sure that she gets there safely."

"Why will you not take her?"

"I need to stay in the valley to protect it from Smith."

"I know of Smith. He is mean."

"Yes, he is. Will you help me?"

"Yes. I know a way to the stage stop so she will not be seen by anyone."

"Good."

"When do you wish for me to take her to the stage stop?"

"As soon as possible."

"I will go with you now. We can leave soon. I will be making a stop at my camp on the way. My woman will want to know where I am going."

"Good," Frank said, then turned his horse around. Red Owl rode up beside Frank as they rode back to the mine.

As soon as they arrived at the mine, Frank introduced Susan to Red Owl and explained what they were going to do. Even though it concerned Susan, they packed what Susan would need for a stay in Custer City. Frank also gave her what money he had to pay for food and lodging while in Custer City.

Susan signed a note stating that Frank had a right to be on her property. Frank saddled Susan's horse and handed the reins of the other two horses to Red Owl.

"Red Owl will take you to Four Mile Stage Stop. From there you will go on to Custer City where you will find the sheriff and tell him what is going on here. Tell him everything that has happened here. Don't forget to tell him that I am here protecting your ranch."

"Our ranch," she corrected him.

"Our ranch," he said with a smile.

Susan stepped into the saddle of her horse and looked down at Frank. She leaned down and kissed him.

"Be careful," she said.

"You, too. You better get going. I'd like you to get to the stage stop before dark," Frank said.

Susan nodded then touched the side of her horse in the ribs. The horse started to move.

Frank stood there and watched as Red Owl led Susan away from the mine. As soon as they were out of sight, Frank took a look around. He was just looking to see if anyone had come into the valley. He saw no one.

# CHAPTER EIGHTEEN

Susan rode a little behind Red Owl as they moved through the forest toward the upper end of the valley. She wondered where he was taking her. She even began to wonder if she should trust him. Susan had never been to the upper end of the valley and had no idea what was in that area.

They hadn't gone very far when she took a second to look back toward where the mine was located. She could not see it. The further away from the mine they went, the more she thought about leaving the valley. She wondered if leaving the valley had been a good idea, but she would trust Frank's judgement.

Time passed slowly as they continued to go farther and farther away from the valley, but never once leaving the forest. Susan suddenly realized that if Red Owl left her once they were out of the valley, she might not be able to find her way back. It was a scary thought that he might not be taking her to the stage stop.

After several hours of travel, they suddenly came to a clearing alongside a creek. In the clearing were a dozen or more tepees. She began to realize that Red Owl had taken her to his village.

As they approached, a number of women and children came out to greet Red Owl, along with several Indian braves. The sight of all the Indians frightened her as she remembered all the stories she had heard about what Indians did to white women.

Red Owl drew up and slid off his pony. He reached up and took hold of the reins of Susan's horse. He motioned for her to get off the horse.

Susan hesitated for a moment, but quickly understood that she really didn't have a choice. She got down from the horse and just stood there looking at all the Indians who were looking at her.

"We will get something to eat before we go onto the stage stop," Red Owl said.

Red Owl turned and started walking toward a tepee that had a large pot hanging over a fire in front of it. He was greeted by an Indian woman as she came out of the tepee. He talked briefly to the woman, then turned and motioned for Susan to come closer. Once she was standing near them, Red Owl again spoke to her.

"This is my woman. We will eat here, then go on to the stage stop."

The woman took two bowls, filled them with venison stew from the large pot. She gave one to her husband and one to Susan. She then filled a bowl for herself. As soon as they all had a bowl, they sat on a blanket on the ground near the fire and ate.

While they were eating, Red Owl explained to his wife, in the Lakota language, the language of the Sioux, about the smoke they had seen, and that the woman's cabin and barn had been burned down by white men to force her and her man out of the valley. He also told her the woman's man gave him the two horses in exchange for seeing that Susan got to the Four Mile Stage Stop safely.

Red Owl's woman looked at the other woman, then at her husband and smiled. She said something to her husband that Susan did not understand. Red Owl could tell that Susan didn't understand.

"My woman said you are a very lovely young woman, and she hoped all will be well with you and your man."

"Would you please tell her 'thank you' for me? It is nice of her to wish us well."

Red Owl told his woman in their language what Susan had said. He turned, looked at Susan, then handed his empty bowl to his woman and stood up.

"We must go or it will be dark before we get to the stage stop," he said to Susan.

Susan stood, handed the bowl to Red Owl's woman then thanked her. She then followed Red Owl to the horses and got in the saddle. As soon as Red Owl said goodbye to his woman, they headed out again.

It was slow going as they moved through the forest. From what Susan could tell, Red Owl had taken a long way around in an effort to miss Smith's ranch and to avoid being seen by Smith or any of his ranch hands. If she was seen, they would know that she had not died in the fire.

After Red Owl and Susan had left, Frank picked up his rifle and started out away from the mine. He first walked up behind the mine, then began walking around the perimeter of the valley, staying well inside the woods to avoid anyone seeing him while still being able to see into the open part of the valley from between the trees. He took his time and kept his eyes moving in the hope of seeing anyone who might be around before they saw him. He was hoping that the forest was not hiding anyone who might want to do him harm.

As he moved through the forest, he kept an eye out for any fresh tracks that would tell him if someone was around. It would take him the better part of the day to make it all the way around the valley on foot as he was moving slowly while staying in among the trees.

When he got to the lower end of the valley, he took time to check the long narrow canyon that his horse had brought him through. He checked to see if there were any fresh tracks in the narrow canyon. He found none.

Frank moved on around the edge of the valley. He continued his search for tracks. The only ones he found were from deer and elk. He found a few from big horn sheep, but none from shod horses or men's boots.

He made his way all the way to behind the barn where he found a lot of tracks from shod horses and men with boots. It was where Smith and his men had come into the valley to attack them, and burned the cabin and barn. In checking out the tracks, he found they had used the same buffalo trail Susan and Frank had used to get to his ranch house. The tracks also showed they had left the same way they had come.

Although Susan and Frank had already decided to rebuild, Frank spent some of his time looking for a place in the valley where they might want to rebuild the cabin and barn, instead of rebuilding it at the old site. He found what he thought would be a better place to rebuild. He would talk it over with Susan as soon as their war with Smith was over.

It was getting dark by the time Frank got back to the mine. He made sure the tarps were closed tight so the glow of a fire could not be seen by anyone. He cooked his meal, then sat down and ate it. After letting his cooking fire die down to a few coals, he built a fire in the little stove inside the mine to warm it.

He didn't bother to take off his clothes when he laid down to sleep. He wanted to be ready for anything. With his horse just out in front of the mine, he was sure that if anyone or anything came around, the horse would let him know. It wasn't long before he was asleep.

The sun was just beginning to set over the distant hills when Red Owl and Susan rode out of the woods and started across an open field toward the Four Mile Stage Stop. John had been standing out on the front porch, leaning against a pole while smoking his pipe. He was looking around before he was going to turn in for the night when he saw two riders coming out of the woods on the other side of the meadow.

He couldn't tell who they were. He called for Mary to join him on the porch.

"Mary, you might want to come out here. We got company," John said.

"Who'd be comin' here at this hour," Mary said as she stepped out on the porch.

"Don't rightly know, but I think one of 'um's a woman."

"I think you're right," Mary said as they came closer.

As they came closer to the stage stop, Mary recognized the woman.

"Why it's Susan McDonald. I wonder what she's doing out here," Mary said.

"That's an Indian with her. It looks like Red Owl. Now, what would she be doing with an Indian?" John said.

"Somethin' must have happened," Mary said with a concerned looked on her face.

It was only a few minutes before Red Owl and Susan stopped in front of the porch. Mary and John waited while Susan got off her horse and stepped up on the porch. Red Owl remained on his horse.

"For land sakes, what are you doing out here." Mary asked. "You look tired. Come inside, I'll fix you something then you can tell me what's goin' on."

Susan went inside the stage stop with Mary right behind her.

"Red Owl, you get down and come inside, too," John said.

Red Owl nodded, got off his horse and tied it to the hitching rail, then stepped up on the porch. Red Owl followed John into the stage stop and sat down on a chair that John pointed at.

Susan sat down on a chair and began telling Mary and John her story. They were surprised to hear that Jacob had been murdered, but not all that surprised when she told them that he had been murdered by Smith, or some of his men. He was well known to be a mean and forceful man with little patience when it came to getting what he wanted.

She told them about Smith and his men burning down her cabin and barn, and about Frank Griswold who had come to help her. She left nothing out.

"I'm going into Custer City to get the sheriff," she said.

"The stage won't be here until mid-afternoon," John said.

"I don't want to wait that long. I need to get to the sheriff as soon as I can," Susan said.

"You spend the night here. In the morning, John will ride with you to see the sheriff," Mary said. "Red Owl, you can stay here tonight, too. It's not safe to travel in the mountains at night."

Red Owl didn't answer her, he simply nodded his head.

After Susan and Red Owl had had something to eat, Susan was shown where she was to sleep. Red Owl insisted that he sleep outside on the porch.

John and Red Owl went outside. They walked the horses to the barn where they rubbed them down and fed them. When all was done, they returned to the stage stop where Red Owl laid out his blanket on the porch while John went inside.

It was shortly before the sun came up over the Black Hills east of Four Mile Stage Stop when John stepped out on the front porch. He looked to the side where Red Owl had laid out his blanket. He noticed that Red Owl's blanket was gone. He was not surprised, and suspected that Red Owl's horse was probably gone as well.

John went to the barn where Red Owl's horse had been. It was gone. He saddled Susan's horse and one for himself and led them to the front of the stage stop. He had just tied the horses to the hitching rail when Susan came out. She saw her horse was saddled and ready to go.

"Thank you for getting my horse for me."

"No problem. Mary and I talked about it last night. I'm going to ride into Custer City with you."

"You don't need to do that."

"I know, but we would feel better if you didn't go alone."

"Okay. Mary asked me to tell you that breakfast is on the table."

"Well, let's get something to eat before we go," John said as he stepped up on the porch and followed Susan into the stage stop.

Susan had breakfast with the Millers. As soon as they were done, John and Susan got on their horses and headed for Custer City to talk to the sheriff.

# CHAPTER NINETEEN

Susan and John arrived in Custer City about noon and went directly to the sheriff's office without stopping for lunch. A note on the door told them the sheriff was across the street at the café having his lunch. Susan and John went across the street to the local café and found Sheriff Metcalf sitting at a table eating. Susan and John walked up to the sheriff. The sheriff looked up at them.

"Sheriff, I need to talk to you," Susan blurted out.

"Why don't the two of you sit down and tell me what's on your mind. I saw you ride into town. You might as well have something to eat, since you're here. You look like you've come a long way," the sheriff said.

John held out a chair for Susan then waited for her to sit down. He then pulled up a chair and sat down next to her.

"Two of the specials for my friends," the sheriff called out to the waitress.

"What's on your mind?" the sheriff said as he took another bite of his roast beef then looked at them. "And why don't you start out by telling me who you are, I already know John."

"I'm Susan McDonald. My husband - - .

"I know who your husband is. Did he come into town with you?" the sheriff asked then took another bite of his meal.

"No. My husband is dead, and he was killed by Wilbur Smith."

Susan's statement caused Sheriff Metcalf to stop chewing in the middle of a bite and looked at her. From the look on her face, he could tell that she was serious. He finished chewing and swallowed what he had in his mouth, then leaned back and looked at her while he wiped his mouth.

"Are you sure it was Smith who killed your husband?"

"Yes. The very next day he came to my cabin to get me to leave my valley ranch. He threatened me. Oh, he didn't come right out and say it, but it was clear what he meant. He also stole two of my horses when he had Jacob beaten to death, then stole what little livestock I had."

"Are you sure he stole your horses?"

"Yes, I'm sure," Susan said thinking that he might not believe what she was telling him.

"That's a pretty serious accusation, Mrs. McDonald," the sheriff said.

"That's not the half of it. He and his men burned down my cabin and barn. And before you ask, I have a very good witness. Mr. Frank Griswold saw Smith give the order to his men to burn me out, and that he didn't care if I was in the cabin. As far as I know, Mr. Smith thinks I died in the fire. It happened the day before yesterday in the morning. They thought I was in the cabin when they burned it to the ground. He even went so far as to have his men surround the cabin and barn to make sure that I didn't get out," she explained angrily.

"Frank Griswold saw all of it?" the sheriff asked looking at her as if he doubted her story.

"Yes. We don't know for sure, but Frank thinks that one of Smith's men shot him when he was on his way to my valley ranch to see if I was all right."

"Is Frank all right?"

"Yes, he's doing fine."

"I know Frank Griswold. What reason did Frank have for going to your ranch in the first place? Did you send for him?"

"No, I didn't send for him. He told me that while he was in a saloon in Cheyenne, some cowboy told him I was alone. He came to see if I was okay, and to see if what the cowboy had told him was true. Frank said he thought the cowboy knew something about the beating death of my husband and the theft of my horses, but the cowboy denied it. Frank was shot, twice, on his way to my valley ranch."

"When did this all happen?"

"It started a little over a month ago when they killed my husband, but the burning down of my cabin and barn was just the other day. Before my husband was beaten and killed, he told me about Smith trying to buy him out, but he wouldn't sell to him."

"I find it hard to believe that Mr. Smith would kill your husband and try to kill you for your valley ranch."

"Believe it or not, he did. He is not only the murderer of my husband, he stole two of our horses and stole our cattle, about two dozen of them. What are you going to do about it?" Susan asked, demanding an answer.

"I'm going to go out there and have a talk with Smith," the sheriff said, not really liking her demanding that he do something.

"Have a talk with him! That's it? What kind of a lawman are you?"

"Listen, Little Lady," the sheriff said sharply. "I'm a damn good lawman. I don't arrest someone unless I have enough proof to do so. When I arrest someone, they don't get out of my jail until a judge tells me to let 'um go, or I take them to the Territorial Prison, or I hang 'um."

It was clear she had not helped her case any by making the sheriff angry. She took a deep breath and looked at John for a moment. She turned back and looked at the sheriff.

"I'm sorry. It's just that I have been under a lot of stress," Susan said, then went on to tell him everything that had been going on at her valley ranch.

"I understand. It's time to leave this to me. Do you have someplace to stay?"

"Frank gave me enough money to stay in Custer City for a day or two," she replied.

"By the way, where is Frank now?"

"He is keeping an eye on our valley ranch while I'm here."

The sheriff noticed that she said "our valley ranch", but chose not to comment on it.

"With the cabin and barn burned down, where is he sleeping?"

"Jacob had lived in an old mine back in the woods a little ways from where he had built the cabin and barn. It is hidden very well in the woods. Frank is staying in the mine."

"I'll go out and have a talk with Smith. I would like to see what he has to say about all of this. I want you to stay away from there for a while. Do you have some place you could stay for a couple of days?"

"She can stay with Mary and me at the stage stop. We plan to leave in the morning and return there."

"That would be good. I will leave first thing in the morning. I don't want you anywhere near your ranch until I have finished talking to Smith. Do you understand?"

"Yes. What about Frank? Smith doesn't know he has been there helping me."

"Smith thinks you have been living there all alone?" Sheriff Metcalf asked with a hint of surprise in his question.

"Yes. We made a point of not letting him know that Frank was there, especially at first when Frank was injured and couldn't get around very well."

"I won't say anything to Smith about Frank, but I will try to talk to Frank if I can see him without Smith knowing it. I'll be leaving at sunup. I don't want you to ride with me. I don't want any of Smith's ranch hands to know that I've even talked with you. By the way, were your cattle branded?"

"Yes, they were."

"What about the horses?"

"Jacob had branded the horses as well with a small 'JM' on their left flank. The two horses were work horses we used to pull our wagon. They were a matched pair, dark brown with white stockinged front feet. In the bright sun, they look sort of reddish brown."

"Thank you. That should help identify the horses if I see them. You get some rest and don't leave until about nine in the morning. That will give me a good head start," the sheriff said.

"Thank you," Susan said, feeling a little relieved that someone was going to try to put a stop to Smith's activities.

Susan watched as the sheriff stood up and left the café. She turned her attention to the roast beef dinner that had been set in front of her. She wasn't very hungry, but she thought she should eat something. She turned her head and looked at John only to discover that he was looking at her.

"Do you think it will do any good for the sheriff to talk to Smith?" she asked.

"I wouldn't count on it. He'll have his men swear that he had nothing to do with it."

"I wish I could find the young cowboy that told Frank about me being alone. Frank seems to think he was there when Jacob was beaten and our horses were taken."

"It would be my guess the young cowboy is well out of the area, probably out of the territory, with no intentions of returning."

"I'm sure you're right," Susan said then turned her attention back to the meal in front of her.

After Susan and John had finished their meal, they went for a walk around town. John picked up a couple of things at the general store that Mary said she wanted him to get. Susan just looked around the store while John shopped.

Since Susan didn't feel much like shopping, she left John at the general store. She told him she would meet him for dinner at the hotel about six. Once she was in her room, she laid down on the bed. She wondered what Frank was doing and if he was safe.

Susan thought about what would happen tomorrow when the sheriff talked to Smith. It took her awhile before she could clear her mind enough to take a nap.

It was almost six in the evening when Susan woke up. She took a few minutes to get ready, then went down to the dining room of the hotel where she found John seated at a table near the front window. John stood up as she approached the table then sat back down as soon as she sat down.

"I hope you got some rest," John said.

"I must have, I slept for almost four hours. The bed was very comfortable."

"What are your plans for tonight?"

"I thought I would get a newspaper and see what has been going on around here. It has been a long time since I've even seen a newspaper," Susan said with a smile.

"I'm sure it has. I doubt you will find our Custer Weekly Chronicle newspaper as exciting as the big Chicago newspapers."

"I don't know. Sometimes a small town newspaper has some rather interesting stories in them," she said with a smile.

John and Susan sat at the table and talked while having a rather leisurely dinner. When dinner was over, Susan excused herself, picked up a copy of the local newspaper at the hotel's front desk and took it to her room. She sat at a small table next to the window and read the newspaper before she turned in for the night.

When morning came, Susan was up with the sun. Since she had a couple of hours before she was to leave Custer City, she sat down at the table and looked out the window. There didn't seem to be very much going on so early in the morning. She did see a large freight wagon drawn by four teams of oxen turning around in the very wide street. It took a while for the wagon master to get the oxen to turn the wagon around.

A movement down the street a little ways caught her eye. It was Sheriff Metcalf on his horse and he was headed west out of town. Susan was sure that the sheriff was on his way out to "have a talk" with Smith.

As he passed under her window, she thought about what he was going to do. She remembered what John had said about doubting his talk with Smith would do any good. About the only thing she could do at this point was to wait and see what came of it.

Susan took her time at getting ready to go downstairs to have breakfast in the hotel dining room. When she arrived in the dining room, she found John sitting at a table reading the newspaper. He put the newspaper down and stood up when he saw her walking across the room toward him.

"I hope you slept well," John said as he pulled out a chair for her.

"Yes, I did," she replied as she sat down at the table.

It wasn't long before a young girl came to their table and got their order for breakfast. As soon as it arrived, they ate without talking. It seemed they both had a lot on their minds. John spoke first after they finished eating.

"Are you anxious to get back to your ranch?"

"Yes, I am. I'm a little worried about Frank, ah, Mr. Griswold."

"I've known Frank for a good many years. He's probably the most honest man I've ever met."

"That's nice to hear," Susan said with a smile.

"Is there anything you need to get before we head back to the stage stop?"

"I would like to get a couple of boxes of ammunition for my rifle and shotgun," Susan said.

"We have that at the stage stop. You can get it there."

"In that case, I don't think so. We have plenty of food, at least for awhile."

"I would like to place an order with the owner of the livery stable for feed for the stagecoach horses. Once I have that done we can head back."

"That would be fine."

They paid for their breakfast then left the hotel. They walked to the livery stable and saddled up their horses. While Susan waited, John told the owner of the livery stable what he would need for the stagecoach horses. As soon as they were done, they rode by the general store and on out of town.

Susan could hardly wait to get to the stage stop. The sheriff had made it clear that she was to stay away from valley ranch until he had talked to Smith. She wanted to be sure she was at the stage stop when the sheriff got there after talking to Smith. It took them several hours to get to the stage stop. When they arrived they were met by Mary.

"Sheriff Metcalf stopped by on his way to the Smith ranch. He told me to make sure that you stayed here until he gets back," Mary said.

"I know. He said he was going to have a talk with Smith and would talk to me here," Susan said. "Have you heard anything from Frank?"

"No. Not a word. Was he supposed to come here?" Mary asked with a concerned look on her face.

"No, but I thought he might come by once the sheriff talked to Smith."

"The sheriff stopped by this morning, but only stayed for a minute before he headed for the Smith ranch. I don't expect him back here until this evening. It would take him awhile to get to Smith's ranch and talk to Smith," Mary assured Susan.

Susan just nodded that she understood, but she looked off toward the direction the sheriff would have gone if he was going to Smith's ranch. She was worried he might not find out anything to help her prove her case against Smith.

"Susan, why don't you come on inside and have a cup of coffee," Mary suggested, then Mary looked at John. "John, we have a stage scheduled here within the hour. You might want to get the horses ready for it."

John looked from Mary to Susan then back to Mary. He got the feeling that Mary wanted to be alone with Susan.

John smiled and said, "I'll get the horses ready."

John turned, left the stage stop and walked out to the barn. He gathered the horses in the small corral next to the barn and began putting harnesses on each of the horses. He wanted them ready to change places with the horses that would bring the stagecoach to the stop. When he was done, he took the time waiting for the stagecoach to clean the stalls in the barn.

# CHAPTER TWENTY

It was cold in the mine when Frank woke. The fire in the small stove had gone out. He quickly climbed out of bed and restarted the fire. It didn't take long before the warmth of the fire began to spread out in the mine.

As Frank thought about his day, he couldn't help but wonder if Susan had been able to find Sheriff Metcalf. He was sure Red Owl would get her to the stage station, but he wasn't sure if the sheriff would be in town when she got there. He hoped Susan would wait for the sheriff if he was not there rather than return to the valley. She was safer there.

Frank fixed his breakfast then sat down at the little table to eat. When he was finished, he cleaned up his dishes. It was time to take a look around the valley again, and see if anyone might be snooping around. He saddled up his horse, then carefully pulled opened the tarp to peek outside to see if there was anyone around. When he was sure it was clear, he walked his horse out of the shelter at the entrance of the mine, mounted up and rode away from the mine.

Letting the horse walk through the woods gave Frank time to look around. As he rode around the valley, staying well inside the woods so he could not be easily seen, he looked for any signs that someone had been there. The first signs of horses he found were the tracks of Red Owl's horse, the two horses he had given Red Owl and the horse Susan had been riding. Those tracks headed deeper into the woods toward the upper end of the valley. He smiled at the thought that Red Owl was taking Susan to safety.

He was about half way around the valley when he found tracks from another horse. He had never seen the tracks before, and they were near the lower end of the valley. Frank got down off his horse to take a closer look at the tracks. From the looks of the tracks in the soft dirt, the steel horse shoe of the right front hoof of the horse had a deep grove cut in it. It was a fresh track. He couldn't remember ever seeing that kind of a track before. It immediately heightened his awareness of his surroundings.

Frank took a minute to look in the direction that the tracks indicated the horse had gone. His mind was working hard to figure out where the horse had gone and who might have been on the horse. There was only one way to find out. Frank swung up into the saddle and slowly began to follow the tracks.

It wasn't long before he saw a man on a horse. Since he was behind the man, and he was hard to see in among the trees, Frank was unable to identify him. He reined up and sat on his horse while he watched the man. Whoever was on the horse didn't seem to be in any hurry.

The man got off his horse and tied it to a low hanging branch. He looked around, then suddenly he untied his horse, swung into the saddle and made a mad dash for the narrow canyon that led into the valley.

Frank wasn't sure if the man had seen him or if he had heard something, but he was getting out of the valley as fast as he could. Frank thought about going after the man, but decided against it. If he had been seen, it was probably one of Smith's men and he was going back to the ranch to tell Smith he saw someone in the valley.

Off to the side of where he was sitting on his horse, Frank heard a twig snap. He turned and looked toward where the sound had come from and saw an Indian sitting on a horse. Frank quickly recognized the Indian as Red Owl. Frank turned his horse and rode over to Red Owl.

"It is good to see you, Red Owl."

"I saw the man. He came into the valley a little while ago," Red Owl said.

"How long have you been here?" Frank asked.

"Since sun come up."

"Did you see what he was doing here?"

"No, but he not very good at hiding," Red Owl said with a grin.

"I thought for a moment he had seen me."

"No. He saw me. I wanted him to see me so he would not see you."

"Thank you for that. Do you know who he is?"

"No, but he work for big cattle man over that way," Red Owl said as he pointed off toward the southwest.

Frank knew he was talking about Smith's ranch. He wondered why one of Smith's men would be skulking around the valley ranch. Did Smith think that Susan had someone helping her? If so, was he afraid that the person helping her might have seen them set fire to the cabin and barn?

"You think he knows about you?" Red Owl asked.

"He might, but I don't think so. His boss might have sent him over here to see because he thinks it is possible she had someone helping her. He might just be here to make sure no one moves in on the land."

"He has seen me," Red Owl said with a grin.

"Yes. You can bet he will tell his boss that the only thing he saw was an Indian," Frank said with a smile.

"You want me to keep watch here?"

"It would be nice to have an extra set of eyes watching the valley."

"I will help."

"Thank you. I don't think we will have any problems for awhile."

"I will go on around the other side of the valley, then return to my village. I will come back tomorrow to watch," Red Owl said.

"Thank you."

Red Owl nodded then turned his pony and rode off. Frank watched him as he rode toward the other side of the valley. He had no doubt that Red Owl would report to him anything he saw on that side of the valley.

Frank rode over to the narrow canyon leading into the valley to make sure that the man he had seen earlier had really left. He found the tracks of the horse, and from the looks of them the man had been riding hard to get out of there. Frank smiled to himself, then turned his horse and began riding back through the woods toward the mine.

As he rode behind what was left of the cabin and barn, he looked at the remains. The sight of the remains got him to thinking about what could have happened if they had spent the night in the cabin. His thoughts caused anger to swell up in him. He turned and headed back to the mine.

When he finally got back to the mine, he had formed a plan of attack on Smith's ranch. It would have to be at night. Frank ate his lunch, then got on his horse and rode across the ridge. It was slow going as he didn't want anyone to see him. If he was seen, they might get the idea that he had been in the valley all the time to protect and help Susan.

It took him a long time to get to a place where he could see the ranch house and the surrounding buildings. Frank found a place where he could hunker down and just watch without being seen. His dapple gray horse could just stand there among the trees and not be seen.

Frank hadn't been watching the ranch house very long when he saw a lone rider come riding toward the ranch house. It wasn't until the rider got closer that he recognized him. It was Sheriff Jeff Metcalf of Custer County. It quickly became clear that Susan had found the sheriff and had had a talk with him.

As he watched, Wilbur Smith came out of the ranch house and greeted the sheriff as he reined his horse up in front of the ranch house. The sheriff got off his horse, stepped up on the porch and shook hands with Smith. They talked briefly then went into the house.

It wasn't long before the cook came out of the house and walked over to the bunkhouse. Three of Smith's men came out of the bunkhouse, walked over to ranch house and walked in.

Frank didn't know what was being said, but there was little doubt in his mind that the ranch hands had been called to tell the sheriff a story about the burning of Mrs. McDonald's cabin and barn. Frank had no idea if they were trying to blame the fire on the Indians in the area, or if they were blaming it on an accident. The only thing he was sure of was that the sheriff was not getting the true story of what had happened.

Time passed slowly for Frank as he stayed hidden at the edge of the woods watching Smith's ranch house. It was well over an hour before there was any movement Frank could see. It was only when the door to the ranch house opened that he saw any activity.

Sheriff Metcalf stepped out on the porch followed by Smith and three of his men. Smith and his men stood on the porch while the sheriff shook hands with Smith. The sheriff then stepped off the porch, untied his horse from the hitching rail and mounted up. The sheriff touched the brim of his hat, then swung his horse around and rode off the same way he had come.

From what Frank had seen, he was sure the sheriff had gotten no information that would help him believe anything had happened that would make him want to investigate further.

As far as Frank was concerned, it was time for him to take matters into his own hands. He moved to a place where he could still see the ranch house, but where it would be more comfortable for him to relax while he watched. From where he was he could also see the front door of the bunkhouse.

It had turned dark and the temperature had grown cold. Frank had waited in his hiding place until all was quiet and all the lights had gone out. Leaving his horse where he could easily find him again, he began working his way very carefully down off the hill and toward the ranch house. Putting his bandana over his face, he stepped up on the porch, reached out and tried the door. The door opened without a sound. Frank stepped inside and looked around.

Frank had never been in Smith's ranch house. The only thing that gave off any kind of light was the glow of the fire place, but it was enough. He noticed that there was a bow with two arrows hanging above the fireplace. He smiled as he looked at it, then very carefully took the bow and arrows down. Frank moved to the door he was sure led to Smith's bedroom. Being as careful and as quiet as he could, he stuck one of the arrows in the door to the bedroom. He could hear Smith snoring; so he was sure he had the right door and he hadn't awakened him. He then left the ranch house, closing the door quietly behind him.

He then moved to a place where he could quickly disappear into the woods, but still see the door to the bunkhouse. Taking careful aim at the door to the bunkhouse, he drew back the bow and fired the arrow into the door of the bunkhouse.

Frank no more than shot the arrow at the bunkhouse when he quickly turned and disappeared into the dark woods. He was almost to his horse when he heard the bunkhouse door open. He turned and saw one of the ranch hands carrying a lantern in one hand while looking outside. Frank quickly ran to his horse. Just as he got to his horse, he heard the ranch hand who had opened the door give an alarm to the others that there was an arrow in the door.

Frank didn't wait around to find out what happened, but he was sure there would be a lot of talk before they would take any action. He also knew Smith would be surprised to find an arrow in his bedroom door.

Frank took his time leaving the area. He didn't want anyone in the ranch house yard to hear him. When he was far enough away, he moved a little faster, but not so fast as to cause him to run into a tree branch or his horse to trip in a hole. Once he got back to the mine, he took care of his horse, then built a fire in the stove. Once it was going well, he went to bed. Having been out in the cold for so long, it took him awhile to get warm enough to go to sleep.

It was late in the afternoon when Susan saw Sheriff Metcalf coming toward Four Mile Stage Stop. She had been waiting on the porch for him. She was very much interested in what Smith might have told him. She stood up as he reined up his horse, then stepped out of the saddle and tied his horse to the hitching rail.

"Well, what did you find out?" Susan asked.

"Not much I'm afraid. Smith said he had nothing to do with your husband's death, or any threats to you, or the burning down of your cabin or barn. He had witnesses to back him up."

"That was what I would have expected him to say. Did you look for my horses?"

"No. I can't just go in, search a man's property and accuse a man of something without some kind of evidence to back it up. It just ain't right."

"So you don't plan to do anything about it. Is that right?" Susan said angrily.

"That's it, unless you can provide me with some proof," the sheriff said.

"Did you even go look at what was left of my cabin and barn?"

"No need for that. What would it show me? About all there would be is a burned down cabin and barn. There'd be nothin' to prove who done it."

"There would be tracks that showed whoever did it came from Smith's ranch," Susan said.

"They wouldn't tell me who it was that burned down your cabin only that they came from the direction of Smith's Ranch."

"Did you talk to Frank?"

"No. I didn't go to your ranch. I couldn't very well go there without Smith knowing it."

Susan looked at him with a discussed look on her face. It had become clear that Frank and she were going to have to take matters into their own hands. The only law they would have was the law they could dish out themselves. With that thought clearly set in her mind, she turned around sharply and walked into the stage stop.

John had been standing next to the door listening to what they had to say. He could certainly understand Susan's feelings at the moment.

"You need a cup of coffee, sheriff?" John asked.

"No. I think I better head back to Custer City. I got a lot to do. Nothing more I can do here, at least for now."

"Okay, but I think you should at the very least go to her ranch and see what was done there. You might find something that would tell you who did it. Besides, it'll be dark soon. You can stay here and go with her in the morning. It might give you a chance to talk to Frank."

The sheriff took a minute to think about what John had said. He had a point. In fact, he had several good points. There was a possibility that there might be some evidence that would point to who had burned down her cabin and barn, and maybe something to support her claim that Smith killed her husband. It might also give him a chance to talk to Frank.

"I'll take you up on your offer. I'll stay and go with her to her valley ranch in the morning," the sheriff said.

The sheriff left the porch, untied his horse and walked it over to the barn.

Meanwhile, Susan was inside sitting at a table with Mary looking depressed and angry.

"What are you going to do now?" Mary asked.

Susan looked up at her and said, "I'm going back to my valley ranch and get my cattle and horses back from Smith, or die trying."

"Do you think that's wise?"

"Probably not, but it is the only place that I can call my own. Frank is there. He will want to know what the sheriff said."

"Do you know your way back?" Mary asked.

"I'll find my way back," Susan said sharply with a hint of determination in her voice.

"You best wait for morning. If you lose your way, you could end up going in circles in the dark."

After taking care of his horse for the night, the sheriff returned to the stage stop and went inside for the cup of coffee he had been offered.

John smiled as he followed the sheriff inside. Sheriff Metcalf saw Susan was sitting at a table with Mary. She looked up and saw the sheriff.

"I decided to stay and go with you to your valley ranch," the sheriff said with an apologetic tone in his voice. "I want to see the damage that was done. I wouldn't be doing my job if I didn't at least take a look around to see what I can find. Besides, I want to have a talk with Frank. If it's all right with you, we'll leave in the morning."

Susan could hardly believe her ears. He was actually going to her valley ranch.

"Thank you so much. Leaving in the morning would be fine," Susan said, almost instantly feeling better.

"I know I feel a lot better knowing that you will not have to travel alone," Mary said.

"So do I," Susan admitted.

"Well, for now, we'll have something to eat, then you can get a good night's sleep," Mary said.

Susan helped Mary get dinner ready. Once it was ready they all sat down to eat. After dinner John and the sheriff went outside for a smoke, while Susan and Mary cleaned up the kitchen. When they were done, they all turned in for the night. It was not easy for Susan to fall asleep as she had a lot on her mind, but sleep finally did come.

# CHAPTER TWENTY-ONE

Smith was awakened by the commotion over by the bunkhouse. He heard the bunkhouse door slam shut and someone calling for the other ranch hands to come quickly. Smith crawled out of bed and went to the window. He could see the bunkhouse from his bedroom window.

What he saw surprised him. There were several of his ranch hands holding up lanterns in one hand while holding a gun in the other and looking around as if they were looking for someone or something. Smith opened the window and called out.

"What's going on out there?"

"It looks like we've had a visitor, Mr. Smith. Someone shot an arrow into the bunkhouse door," Jesse said. "I think they're gone now. I don't see anyone around."

"An arrow? What kind of arrow?"

"I don't know, but it looks a lot like the ones you have hangin' over your fireplace," Jesse said.

Smith looked at Jesse for a moment as if he didn't believe him, then turned and looked at the door to his bedroom. He hadn't seen any arrows like the ones over his fireplace for many years. In fact, he hadn't seen any since he got those arrows and the bow after he raided the Indian encampment shortly after he started his ranch. He thought he had killed all the Indians and taken all the weapons he could find including knives, rifles, bows and arrows, and a couple of pistols.

It suddenly occurred to him that it might be a good idea if he took a look at his fireplace. He didn't think the arrow in the bunkhouse door would be one of the arrows from there, but the thought that it might be was strong. He had to look just to make sure.

Smith walked over to the bedroom door and pulled it open. His eyes got big and his mouth fell open when he saw an arrow sticking in his bedroom door. He instantly looked at the space above the mantle on the fireplace. The bow and the two arrows were gone. It was clear the arrows were the ones stuck in the doors.

"Jesse, get the hell in here," Smith yelled.

It was only a matter of seconds before Jesse came rushing in the door. The first thing he noticed was the look on Smith's face. It was as if he had seen a ghost.

"What is it?" Jesse asked.

"Take a look above the fireplace. What do you see?"

Jesse looked above the fireplace then turned to look back at his boss. He saw that the bow and arrows were missing, but wasn't sure what to say. All he said was, "Nothing."

"That's right. But there is supposed to be a bow and two arrows up there."

"Right."

"One of those arrows is in my bedroom door. I'd be willing to bet that the other one is the one you found in the bunkhouse door. Someone was in my house. The bow and arrows were on that wall above the fireplace when I went to bed," Smith said, angry that someone had walked right into his house, took his bow and shot the arrows into the doors.

"Yes, sir," was all Jesse could think of to say.

"Do you have any idea who came into my house and stole my bow and stuck the two arrows in the doors?"

"No, sir," Jesse said softly, not wanting to upset his boss any more than he was already.

Up to now, Smith had not even thought about the fact that whoever had come into his ranch house could have just as easily killed him in his sleep, and walked away without anyone knowing about it until he was found dead in his bed in the morning.

When the thought that he could have been murdered in his bed finally started to soak in, it scared him half to death. A feeling of panic washed over Smith like he had never felt before. His heart beat rapidly and his breath caught. It took a moment or two before he began to calm himself enough to breathe normally.

After a couple of deep breaths, Smith began to wonder why he wasn't killed. Was the arrow in his door there to show him how vulnerable he was even in his own home? It was suddenly not hard for him to believe he was vulnerable.

"You think whoever done it was tryin' to send you a message, boss?" Jesse asked cautiously in the hope of not upsetting his boss.

Smith looked at his foreman while he thought about what Jesse had said. That was certainly something to think about.

"Any idea who might have done it?" Jesse asked when he didn't get an answer to his first question.

Jesse's questions made Smith think about who might want him dead. He had made a lot of enemies over the past years, but most of them were dead or had left the country. The most current enemy of his was Mrs. McDonald, but she was dead, or was she, he thought.

"Are you sure Mrs. McDonald died in the cabin fire?" Smith asked, looking directly at his foreman with suspicion in his eyes.

"We had the cabin and barn surrounded. There weren't no way anyone could have gotten out of them buildings without us seein' 'um. You don't think any of the hands would have let her escape?"

"Right now, I don't know what to think. That woman was the only one I could think of who might have the guts to try something like this.  But if she died in the fire, who else would have done it?" Smith said thoughtfully.

"Got me.  Maybe it was an Indian, you know, from that tribe you attacked when you first settled here," Jesse suggested.

Smith just looked at his foreman as he thought about what he had said.  The attack on the Indian tribe when he first settled there was a long time ago.  It didn't seem to make sense to him that they would wait so long to seek revenge, yet it was something he could not dismiss from his mind easily.

"I want guards posted on my front porch and in front of the bunkhouse.  I want you to talk to the men and see if any of them have seen any Indians lately, or anyone else that might be hanging around here who they don't know.  That includes the McDonald ranch."

"Yes, sir," Jesse said then turned and left for the bunkhouse.

Smith watched as Jesse left the ranch house.  His mind was working hard in an effort to figure out who stole his bow and shot his arrows into the doors.  He walked over to his chair near the fireplace and sat down.  For the first time since he was a boy, he was actually afraid.  It had been several decades since anyone had had the nerve to challenge him, that was until Mrs. McDonald had come onto his ranch and took a shot at him.

It was the thought of Mrs. McDonald, and the fact she had shot at him and demanded the return of her horses and cattle, that caused him to wonder if Mrs. McDonald might have escaped the fire.  He had been there when they burned down the cabin and barn.  His men had encircled both buildings.  Jesse was right, she would not have been able to escape.  Then it hit him.  Was it possible that she wasn't even in the cabin when they set fire to it?

His thoughts were disturbed when he heard the front door of the ranch house open. He turned and saw Jesse and one of the other ranch hands walk in. He was curious as to what they wanted.

"Mr. Smith, this here is Will Sanders. He's got somethin' to tell you."

"What is it?" Smith demanded, looking at Sanders.

"Well, sir, I was over in the valley where that lady had her cabin and barn burnt down," he said then paused.

"Well, what about it," Smith said impatiently.

"Well, sir. I seen an injin' back in that valley. He was back in some trees away from the open part of the valley."

"Any idea what he was doing there?"

"No, sir. He was just settin' on a brown and white Indian pony lookin' at me and not movin' a muscle."

"Have you ever seen him before, or the horse?"

"No, sir. I ain't never seen him before. And I can tell you, I hope I never see him again."

Smith looked from the ranch hand to his foreman. He wondered what the Indian was doing in the valley. He wondered if it had been the Indian who had come in his ranch house and stole the bow and shot the arrows into the doors.

"By the way, did the Indian have a bow and some arrows?"

"Not that I noticed, but he could have had 'um," Will said, then added, "I did see he had himself a rifle. He had it layin' across his lap kinda relaxed like. You know, like he weren't worried about there bein' any trouble comin' his way."

"Yeah, I know what you mean. You can go," Smith said.

Will and Jesse turned to leave, but Smith told Jesse to stay. As soon as Will had gone, Smith told Jesse to sit down. Jesse walked over to a chair and sat down.

"Do you think he is telling the truth?"

"I don't think he has any reason to lie. When I asked if anyone had been over in the valley, one of the hands told me Will had been over there yesterday morning."

"Was he one of those who had set the cabin and barn on fire?"

"No, sir. As far as he knows, it was just a fire."

"Any idea why he was over there?"

"He went lookin' for stray cattle. He rode up the narrow canyon that leads into the valley lookin' for strays and saw the Indian. He said when he saw the Indian, he got the hell out of there," Jesse explained.

"Did you post guards out?"

"Yes, sir."

"Okay. You can go get some rest. I'm going to turn in. Keep guards around the ranch house and bunkhouse all the time, at least until we figure out what is going on."

"Yes, sir," Jesse said then stood and left the ranch house.

Smith closed and barred the front door as soon as Jesse left then went to his bedroom. He laid down on the bed, but he didn't go to sleep right away. His mind was busy trying to think of who might have entered his home. The fact he could have easily been murdered in his bed played on his mind for a long time before he finally drifted off to sleep, but he got very little rest.

When morning came, Smith dragged himself out of bed. It had been a long night without getting very much rest. He had tossed and turned the entire night, and his mind was filled with thoughts of the Indian Will had seen at the valley ranch.

Smith could hear the cook working in the kitchen. Since he was sure he would not get any more rest, he dressed then went to the dining room for his breakfast and sat down. The cook brought in his usual breakfast and set it down in front of him. Instead of starting to eat, he just sat there and stared at the plate.

Smith's thoughts were of the Indian who had been at the valley ranch. He couldn't get the idea out of his mind that the Indian had probably been the one who had entered his ranch house during the night. He couldn't picture Mrs. McDonald having the nerve to enter his ranch house in the middle of the night. Besides, she was dead, or was she? He still wasn't sure.

He got up from the table and went to the front door. He unbarred the door and opened it. He cautiously looked out to make sure it was safe to go out on his porch. When he saw the ranch hand standing on the porch with a rifle in his hands, he decided to step outside.

"Mornin', Mr. Smith," the ranch hand said.

"Morning," Smith replied as he looked around.

"Looks like it's goin' to be a nice day."

"Yeah," was all Smith said, paying little attention to the ranch hand.

Smith looked around, then turned around and went back into the ranch house. He returned to the table and sat down to eat his breakfast. He seemed to feel a little more secure and more like eating since there was a guard right outside his front door.

After he finished eating, he stepped out on the porch and looked around. He didn't see anyone who might cause him harm. Smith stood looking off in the direction of the valley ranch. He began to think about the Indian and wondered what he had been doing in the valley. Had he seen what had taken place there? If he had, would he tell anyone about it?

Smith didn't think the Indian would want to tell anyone about the fire. People would think he, or someone from his tribe, had set the fire and killed Mrs. McDonald.

The more Smith thought about it, the more he thought it would be a good idea to take a couple of the ranch hands who had been involved in the burning and ride over to the valley. He wasn't sure it would help any, but he wanted to make sure no one was moving into the valley, especially Indians. He didn't want a repeat of what had happened when he first moved into the area.

Smith told the guard to tell Jesse he wanted to see him. He went back into the ranch house and waited for Jesse.

"You wanted to see me, boss?" Jesse said as he stepped inside the ranch house.

"Yes. I want you to get four or five of the ranch hands who were involved in burning the buildings in the valley. We're going over there and have a look around. I want to know if that Indian is still hanging around with thoughts of settling down there. If he's there, I want to run him off or kill him. You understand?"

"Yes, sir. Are you going along?"

"Yes, so saddle a horse for me," Smith said.

Smith dismissed Jesse, then went to get a rifle. He made sure it was ready to use. He strapped on his pistol, grabbed up the rifle and went out on the porch to wait for his horse.

Jesse came around the corner of the ranch house leading Smith's horse. He was followed by five other ranch hands.

Smith stepped off the porch, slipped his rifle in the saddle scabbard then took the reins from Jesse. He put his foot in the stirrup and pulled himself up into the saddle. As soon as he was ready, he turned his horse and started up the hill toward the buffalo trail they had used to get to the valley when they burned the cabin and barn to the ground.

Before they had reached the top of the ridge, a thick fog had rolled in from the top of the ridge making it hard to see more than about ten feet. It slowed down their trek to the valley.

# CHAPTER TWENTY-TWO

When Susan woke she could feel a chill in the air. It was still dark outside, but she could hear the sounds of someone cooking in the kitchen. She wrapped herself in the quilt that had been on the bed then went to the window, drew the certain back and looked out. To her surprise she could not even see the barn. It was a grey day with a thick fog that had rolled in during the early morning hours and was hanging over the land. A feeling of disappointment ran through her body. There was no way she would be able to find her way to the valley ranch in the fog, let alone find her way across the open field to where she had come out of the woods with Red Owl on her way to the stage stop. There was nothing else for her to do but get dressed and have breakfast, then wait for the fog to lift.

As soon as she was dressed, she went to the kitchen. The kitchen was warm and there was a coffee pot on the wood burning stove. Mary was at the counter mixing up a batch of pancake batter. The table was set and the bacon was slowly sizzling in a pan on the stove. Mary looked up and saw Susan watching her.

"Good morning. I hope you slept well," Mary said.

"Yes, I did. It doesn't look like I will be going anywhere this morning," Susan said with a disappointed tone to her words.

"No, I afraid not. The fog came in just a few hours ago from the southwest. It could hang in here for most of the day. It often does this time of year. Why don't you sit down and have a good breakfast?" Mary suggested.

With a sigh of disappointment, Susan walked up to the table, then looked over at Mary.

"Is there anything I can do to help?"

"You can pour coffee in the cups on the table. I'll have the pancakes ready in a few minutes. John and the sheriff will be in shortly. They went out to take care of the animals. If they find any eggs this morning, you can have eggs with your pancakes."

"That would be nice," Susan said.

Just as Susan picked up the coffee pot and began to fill the coffee cups, John and Sheriff Metcalf came in with big grins on their faces. John had his hands full of eggs.

Looks like we have eggs for breakfast," Mary said as she took the eggs from John.

As soon as breakfast was ready, they all sat down to eat. When they were finished eating, Susan spent most of the morning helping Mary in the kitchen and looking out the window from time to time to see if the fog had lifted. The Four Mile Stage Stop stayed like an island in the sea of fog for most of the day.

Around noon a stagecoach arrived for a change of horses. The driver of the stagecoach told Susan that if it wasn't for the road, he would not be able to find his way to the stage stop. The visibility was so bad that he couldn't see for more than ten to fifteen feet in front of the lead team of horses, maybe twenty feet at times, but that was rare.

Susan spent a large part of the afternoon reading one of John's books, and wishing that the fog would lift. John and the sheriff spent time talking about Smith and his ranch. The fog didn't lift all day.

Frank woke and immediately rekindled the fire in the small stove. It didn't take long before it was heating the mine. He put on his coat and looked out to see if there was anyone around. He quickly discovered there was a fairly thick blanket of fog lying over the valley and the surrounding area, and it was cold and damp.

The weather was perfect as far as Frank was concerned. Even though it made it hard, if not impossible, to see very far, he could hear in the quiet of the forest and valley. He had a pretty good idea that Smith would get some men together and start looking for the Indian one of his men had seen in the valley yesterday.

In fact, Frank counted on Smith to be impatient as well as hot tempered. He wasn't one hundred percent sure his ranch hand would report the sighting of the Indian to his boss, but with the way he rode out of the valley there was a pretty good chance he would tell his foreman. Frank was counting on the ranch hand to report it to his foreman, and that was almost as good as telling the boss. The foreman would surely tell Smith.

Frank wondered how Smith would react to the bow and arrows missing from above the mantle over his fireplace, and one of the arrows being stuck in his bedroom door. If Smith thought someone had walked into his ranch house without anyone knowing it didn't scare the hell out of him, the arrow in his bedroom door would certainly have worried him a great deal.

After Frank had his breakfast, he went out to the area in front of the mine where he kept his horse. He saddled his horse, put a rifle in the saddle scabbard then mounted. He was glad his horse was a dapple gray. It made it almost impossible for anyone to see the horse in the fog. Frank rode out from under the tarps that covered the entrance to the cave then turned toward the edge of the valley. He rode around to the area just behind where the cabin and barn had been, then sat in among the trees to wait and listen.

Where he was sitting on his horse was not very far from where Smith and his men had come over the ridge when they burned down the cabin and barn. He figured they would come that way again, for two reasons. One, it was a lot shorter than going around and coming up through the narrow canyon. Secondly, going through the canyon to get to the valley would put Smith and his men in a narrow canyon that made it easy for one or two shooters to hold them off, or cut them to pieces before they could get to any kind of cover. There was also the fact that with the fog, it would be hard for them to even find the canyon.

While Frank waited and listened for any sound that would indicate there was someone coming over the ridge, he thought about the Indian the ranch hand had seen. He wondered if Red Owl would return to the valley today. He would have to keep a watch out for him. He didn't want to accidently shoot him.

It wasn't long until Frank thought he heard something. It sounded like a horse stepping on a branch or a twig. He drew his rifle from the scabbard. He slowly and quietly levered a round into the chamber of his rifle then sat very still. The sound had come from very close to the trail Smith and his men had used when they came into the valley earlier.

Patiently, he sat and listened. It was only a moment or two before he heard what sounded like more than one horse picking their way down off the ridge. Slowly and carefully, Frank stepped out of the saddle. He tied his horse to a low hanging branch, then moved away from the horse. He found a place where there were several boulders with large trees growing between them. He positioned himself between the boulders and took a couple of deep breaths. He then waited.

Even though it was fairly cold and the fog covered the area, Frank began to sweat. He had no idea how many men Smith might have brought with him. With that thought, he drew his pistol from his holster, rechecked it then set it on one of the boulders where it was easy to reach. He was as ready as he could be. Now it was time to wait until he could see who was coming over the ridge.

Frank could hear the faint sound of several horses' hooves as they clicked on the rocky ground. As best he could tell, there were at least three, possible four or five. His plan was simple. He would fire at the first one he could identify as one of Smith's ranch hands, then quickly move from one place to another as he fired at the shadows of men on horseback hoping to get at least a couple of them before taking cover in the fog. He would then move to another position before they knew what hit them, and before they had a chance to see who it was shooting at them.

Suddenly, one of the men spoke. He spoke very softly, but Frank still heard him.

"I sure hope this ain't no trap."

"Quiet," one of the riders said.

That was all Frank needed to hear. It made it possible for him to pinpoint where the voices had come from. He set his sights in the area that the voices had come from and readied himself. He watched and waited until he could see the shadowy lines of a horse and rider.

When he could see enough of the first rider to know what he was shooting at, he leveled his rifle and slowly pulled the trigger. As soon as the shot was fired, he grabbed up his pistol and fired several shots as he quickly moved from one position to another. His hope was they would think there was more than one person shooting at them.

As Frank shot and moved, he heard some return fire, but none of it came close to him. He also could hear cries of pain which told him he had hit at least one or two of the riders. The sounds of the chaos quickly died down and all that was left were the sounds of someone in pain.

Frank knew he had injured at least two of the riders, but he still didn't know how many others were out there. He moved deeper into the forest and circled around so he was behind them. He had no idea if they would retreat back the way they had come, but if there were several who were injured, they might take them back to where they could be cared for and wait for another day to come back. They had walked into his trap, but would probably not fall for it again. It wasn't very long before he heard voices again.

"We need to get out of here. We are sitting ducks in this fog."

Frank didn't know who was doing the talking, but he was sure it was not Smith.

"What's the matter with you? They can't see us any better than we can see them."

Frank knew from the sound of the voice that it was Smith talking.

"We don't even know how many there are, but there have to be at least three."

As they talked, Frank closed in on them. He wanted to find out how many men Smith had brought with him. He moved in until he could just barely see Smith hunkered down behind an old tree that had fallen many years ago. He only knew it was Smith from the bulk of the shadow he made in the fog. He was directly behind Smith. He moved back and laid down at the base of a tree where he could still see Smith's outline as nothing more than a very faint shadow.

Frank put his hands to his mouth then in a whispery voice said, "Go away or die."

A soon as he said it, he rolled away from the tree and slide down into a shallow ravine. Frank moved as quietly as possible to another tree along the edge of the ravine where he repeated his message only with a slightly different tone in his voice. He moved again and repeated it again, again with still another tone in his voice. He could no longer see what Smith and his men were doing, but he was sure they were confused and scared, which was what he had in mind.

"I'm getting out of here," one of the ranch hands said. "There's too many of 'um."

"I'm going with you," another ranch hand said.

"Get back here you damn fools," Smith said, but it was too late.

Frank could hear the two men running. When the sound of them running stopped, he could hear two horses running away from the location. He got a glimpse of one of them as he rode by him. He was looking over his shoulder as if the devil himself was after him.

It wasn't but a moment later that he heard another horse running away from the area toward the ridge. Frank still didn't know how many were still in the area. He knew Smith was still around, but he had no idea how many others had come with him.

Frank held his position in the narrow ravine where he had seen the shadow of the one ranch hand. He had not seen the other two who had left. Frank waited and listened. He wasn't sure how long he waited, but it had been fairly long, perhaps thirty minutes or more.

Finally, Frank heard someone move in the underbrush. It didn't sound like they were coming closer to him. It sounded like someone was walking away.

"Get my horse," Smith said. "I think whoever they were, they're gone."

"We going back to the ranch, boss?"

"Yes. We'll never be able to find them in this fog. Get those two on their horses. We'll take them back."

Frank could hear the groaning of two men as they were put on their horses. Frank moved over closer to the trail that Smith and his men had used to get to the valley, then hunkered down behind some boulders and watched as Smith and his men retreated back to the ranch.

As Smith and his men slowly rode by, Frank saw Smith look back over his shoulder and look toward the valley. The expression on Smith's face showed Frank that it wasn't over. The war was not over, yet.

Frank quickly returned to his horse, mounted and followed Smith and his men as they rode along the buffalo trail that went over the ridge. He wanted to make sure they left the valley. As soon as they crossed over the ridge and were well on their way, Frank turned around and started back toward the mine. He was sure they were not likely to return today, but tomorrow he was not so sure about. It was time to organize a plan that would work when Smith and his men decided to try again to take over the valley by force.

Frank returned to the mine, unsaddled his horse, rubbed him down then fed him. As soon as he was done, he went inside the mine and sat down at the table. He spent the better part of the rest of the morning trying to figure out what Smith would do next.

It was getting on toward noon when Frank thought he heard something. His first thought was the fog had lifted while he was inside planning for another attack. He grabbed his rifle and went out in front of the mine. He slowly pulled back the tarp and looked around.

The fog was still pretty thick and made it hard to see anything or anybody who might be in the area. It was only after his eyes and ears adjusted to his surroundings that he saw a shadowy figure on a horse moving slowly through the forest. It wasn't until he got closer that Frank saw who it was. It was Red Owl.

"Red Owl, what brings you here on a day like this?"

"I came because I told you I would be here."

"Thank you for coming, but you didn't need to come here in this kind of weather. Come and eat with me."

Red Owl and Frank went into the mine. Frank noticed Red Owl looking over the mine and the shelter in front of the mine.

"Good hiding place," Red Owl said.

Red Owl and Frank sat down at the small table inside the mine. They talked about Smith and his ranch while Frank prepared a meal of buffalo stew for them. Actually, the stew had been made by Susan. All Frank had to do was to warm it up.

After they had finished eating, they spent the afternoon getting to know each other and exchanging stories about their lives, something Indians like to do when building a relationship. It wasn't long before the subject turned to Smith and his attack on the valley ranch.

"I heard shooting on my way over here," Red Owl said.

"I'm sure you did. Smith came over here to find you."

"Why would he do that?"

"One of his ranch hands saw you yesterday. I think Smith thought you might be planning on moving into the valley now that the buildings have been destroyed."

"Do not wish to be close to him," Red Owl said.

"I doubt he cares at all what you think or what your plans are. He will go after anyone who he thinks will try to move in on the land he wants," Frank said. "There's one other little thing I probably should tell you."

"What little thing?"

"I attacked him at his ranch last night. He had a bow and two arrows hanging above his fireplace. I took the bow and shot an arrow into the front door of the bunkhouse, and stuck the other arrow into his bedroom door. I think it scared him half to death when he realized I had walked into his ranch house without anyone seeing me. Of course, he didn't know it wasn't you that did it. The ranch hand who saw you must have told him about seeing you, and Smith thought it was you who had walked into his ranch house. He came over here to find you and destroy you," Frank explained. "I'm sorry if it causes you any trouble from him."

Red Owl looked at Frank for a moment. Frank hoped that Red Owl would not be too upset with him. Red Owl began to smile, which was a relief to Frank.

"The bow and arrows Smith had belonged to my ancestors. I had heard the story many times about Smith attacking my ancestors and taking all their weapons. It is good to hear the weapons he took were used against him by a white man."

"There is a certain irony in that," Frank said with a grin. "I still have the bow. I will give it to you. It has been away from the place it belongs for too long."

"We no longer use bows and arrows, but it will be nice to have it back. It belonged to my father."

"I'm sorry if I have accidently brought you into our fight. I didn't intentionally do it."

"I understand. We help save the valley ranch for your woman?"

Frank had not expected Red Owl to offer to help keep the valley ranch out of Smith's hands. With Red Owl's help, he just might be able to save the valley ranch.

# CHAPTER TWENTY-THREE

As soon as Smith and his men arrived back at the ranch, Jesse took the two injured men to the bunkhouse and began taking care of them. Both injured men would not be able to work, let alone fight again for sometime.

Smith went directly to his ranch house, leaving his horse out in front for one of the ranch hands to take care of it. When he entered the ranch house, he slammed the door shut. He was mad as hell. He had been forced to return to his ranch like a beaten dog with his tail between his legs.

As far as Smith knew, he had been beaten by a handful of Indians, the same Indians he had beaten two decades ago. It had quickly become clear to him that he had not killed all of them the first time, but he would this time, he vowed silently to himself. He was not about to let them survive this time. He would find their camp and destroy it to the last man, woman and child.

Smith looked at the empty space above the mantel of the fireplace. It was a reminder of how close they had been able to come to him without anyone knowing. It also showed him how vulnerable he was to attack.

Smith walked across the room and sat down at his desk. He pulled out a map he had made of the area almost twenty years ago. He studied the map closely, but found it would not be a lot of help. The map he had made was of his ranch and very little of the surrounding area. He began to realize just how little he actually knew about the area surrounding his ranch, which was reinforced by the fact he had only known of one way in and out of the valley until he followed the buffalo trail over the ridge that had been used by Mrs. McDonald to attack him. Now he knew of two ways in and out of the valley. Over the ridge was one and through the narrow canyon at the lower end of the valley was the other.

He took a moment to think about the two ways into the valley. He decided the best way to trap the Indians in the valley, and completely destroy them, was to attack them from both ways into the valley. He could not let a single one of them escape.

Smith began to smile to himself as he thought about a two prong attack, but the smile quickly left his face when he looked outside and saw that the fog had not lifted. If the fog hung around much longer, he would have to hold off his attack until tomorrow.

It suddenly occurred to him that he should use this time to gather his men and go over his plan with them. Smith got up from his desk and stepped out onto the porch to talk to the ranch hand who was guarding the front of the ranch house.

"Get Jesse in here," Smith ordered.

"Yes, sir," the ranch hand said then took off running toward the bunkhouse.

As soon as the ranch hand left the porch, Smith turned and looked up the hill from where Mrs. McDonald had attacked him and thought about her for a moment. He then turned and went inside the ranch house. It wasn't very long before Jesse was knocking on the ranch house door.

"Come in," Smith ordered sharply.

Jesse opened the door and walked into the ranch house. He saw Smith sitting at his big desk. Smith appeared to be looking, almost studying something in front of him. Jesse didn't say anything. He didn't want to disturb Smith and possibly get yelled at. Finally, Smith turned and looked at Jesse.

"I want you to get the men together. We are not going to let a bunch of Indians take over the valley ranch."

"Are you sure it was Indians that were shooting at us this mornin'?" Jesse asked.

"Who else could it be? Didn't one of the ranch hands say he saw an Indian in the valley?"

"Well, yes sir, he did. But we didn't see no Indians. We didn't see anybody. We was just shot at, and mighty good shooting considering the weather. There was no way to tell who it was shootin' at us."

"Use your head, man. Mrs. McDonald is dead. No one else has been seen in the valley. And, there were at least three shooters spread out along that outcropping of rocks. What does that tell you?"

"I guess you're right," Jesse conceded after giving it a moment of thought. "What's your plan?"

"My plan is to attack the valley from two different directions. Some of the men will enter the valley from the narrow canyon while the others will attack over the ridge. We will trap the Indians in the valley between us," Smith said with a slight grin.

"That will put some of the men in the lower part of the valley, and some of them about half way up the valley on one side. What's to keep them from escaping over the upper end of the valley?" Jesse asked.

"If they try to escape out the upper end of the valley, they will end up trapped in the valley. There is no way out of the valley at the upper end. Once they are trapped, we will kill them all. We won't let a single one of them get away. I won't have to deal with them again, ever."

"You think they are part of the tribe you attacked when you first settled here?"

"Yes. Why else would they take the bow and shoot the arrows into the doors? It was a message to me that they were back."

Jesse wasn't sure what to think, but he was beginning to think Smith was losing his mind. Jesse had not seen any Indians in the area for a very long time. Even the ranch hand who had seen the Indian had reported seeing only one.

There was also the thought that Jesse had never heard of Indians going around leaving messages, warning someone they were going to attack them. If they had wanted revenge, the Indian who had stolen the bow and shot the arrows into the doors could have killed Smith in his sleep when he broke into the ranch house.

"Don't just stand there. Get the men together," Smith demanded.

"Yes, sir," Jesse said, then turned and left the ranch house.

It took Jesse almost an hour to gather the men together in the bunkhouse. He told them what he had been told before they all went to the ranch house. Once they were gathered in the ranch house, Smith got up from his desk and moved to the table.

"Gather around," he said.

The men gathered around the table. With so many in the room, not all of them could see the makeshift map Smith had laid out on the table.

"It seems we have a slight problem in the valley where Mrs. McDonald had been living. It seems there is a small tribe of Indians who have decided to move in and make camp in the valley. Tomorrow morning, we are going into the valley and clean them out. We will kill every one of them so they will never come back again. Do I make myself clear?"

"Do you think it necessary to kill them all?" one of the ranch hands asked.

"We have already seen what has happened. I ran them out twenty years ago, and now they are back. You saw the arrow stuck in the door of the bunkhouse. What does that tell you?"

"It tells me they want a fight," one of the other ranch hands said.

"I think we should give them what they want, don't you?" Smith said.

There was a lot of mumbling among the ranch hands. Smith could see them nodding their heads and hear them talking among themselves that they agreed with what he was saying.

"Okay," Smith said. "Tomorrow we will attack those in the valley. Jesse will take several of you and enter the valley through the narrow canyon at the lower end of the valley. Once outside the canyon, you will spread out and start combing the valley and the woods on both sides. That will force the Indians to move up the valley.

"I will take the rest of the men, and we will move across the ridge along the buffalo trail and come into the valley from behind where the cabin and barn were. That will put us on the Indians' flank. It will force them to continue to move up the valley until there is no place for them to go."

Smith stopped and looked at his men. No one had said anything, but there was a confused look on the face of Randell, one of the older ranch hands.

"Randell, you seem confused. Do you have a problem with the plan?"

"Not really, sir. I was just wonderin' if they might escape out the upper end of the valley."

"There are only two ways in or out of the valley. Since we will be coming at them from the only two ways in or out of the valley, we will have blocked their escape. Does that answer your concerns?"

Smith watched Randell to see if he had accepted his explanation. Randell was nodding his head slightly while he looked at the map on the table.

Randell looked up at Smith, smiled and said, "Yes, sir. It sure does."

"Good. In that case, this meeting is over. Go to the bunkhouse and make sure your weapons are in good working order. Jesse will be joining you shortly to let you know who you will be riding with. You'll also need to get a good night's rest as we will be up before light to give us time to get into position."

"You heard him. Go get ready for a fight," Jesse said.

Jesse watched as the men left the ranch house. As soon as they were gone, Smith sat down at the table with Jesse and gave him his instructions. Jesse was to bring his group of men up through the narrow canyon while Smith would take the rest of the men into the valley from over the ridge.

Once the plan for the attack was finished, Jesse went to the bunkhouse and told each man who he would be riding with.

The ranch hands spent a good part of the rest of the day preparing for the morning. They had a good meal that evening and turned in early.

Red Owl and Frank sat at the table and talked about what they might expect from Smith. It wasn't hard for them to understand that Smith would attack them in force, probably in the early morning hours.

"I think Smith will wait until morning before he attacks us. He got pretty well burned attacking in the fog. He will wait for it to clear before he tries it again," Frank said.

"This fog will last the day," Red Owl assured him. "I should go back to my camp and talk to the others. I will return at sundown."

"How much of a problem would it be to set up a couple of tepees here in the valley, maybe close to where Smith's ranch hand had seen you?"

Red Owl began to grin. There was little doubt Red Owl had figured out what Frank had in mind.

"Let's go to my camp," Red Owl suggested.

Frank quickly agreed. If Red Owl was ready to help him fight for the valley ranch, it would be good to know how many of Red Owl's people he could count on.

Frank saddled up his horse. As soon as they were ready, Red Owl led the way along the edge of the forest toward the upper end of the valley. When they arrived at the upper end of the valley, Red Owl made a sharp turn onto a narrow buffalo trail. They hadn't traveled very far when they came out into a clearing.

With the heavy fog still covering the land, about all Frank could make out was one or two tepees and the glow of a campfire. As they continued to move toward the tepees, more tepees and more campfires came into sight. By the time they had gotten to the center of the clearing, Frank could make out about a dozen tepees and about fourteen men standing around a fire in the middle of the encampment.

Red Owl took time to talk to several of the Indians near the center of the fire. He talked with them for several minutes.

Frank wasn't sure what was going on, but whatever it was there seemed to be a great deal of interest on the part of those around the fire. It wasn't very long before Frank saw Red Owl turn toward him and motion for him to join the others around the large campfire.

Once at the fire, one of the leaders got a peace pipe and lit it. He then passed it around the circle of men inviting Frank to join them in smoking the peace pipe. Frank had watched how each of them handled the pipe. When it came to him, he knew how to show the respect necessary to avoid upsetting any of them.

After much formality, they began discussing the situation in the valley. Red Owl did most of the talking at first, explaining the situation and what Frank had already done with regard to his fight to keep the valley for him and his woman. He soon turned the talk over to Frank so he could explain what he wanted them to do.

"I have respect for you and your land. My woman and I have been fighting to keep the valley out of the hands of Smith. He has tried to force us to leave, but we will not leave. I know he had forced you away from his ranch many years ago. I would like your help to stop him from taking the valley from us. It would be your chance to get even with him for what he did to your ancestors."

"He has many men and many guns," one of the leaders said.

"Yes, he does. But you have guns, too, and you have the advantage," Frank said.

"How do we have the advantage?" one of the braves asked.

"He doesn't know how many of you there are. He also doesn't know that I exist. I fought in the white man's Great War back east. I was a great leader and fought many battles. You have fought in many battles, too. Smith has not fought in any of the great battles, and he has only cowboys to fight for him, not trained fighters. We also know the area. He will be greatly surprised by the number of us."

There was a great deal of discussion among the leaders as they considered what Frank had said. Red Owl got into the discussion and told them about what Frank had done all by himself that very morning.

Frank sat by and listened. He knew little of their language, but it was clear that Red Owl was trying to convince them to join in, and that Frank and his woman would welcome them at their ranch.

Finally, the discussion ended. Red Owl turned and looked at Frank and smiled.

"They will help," Red Owl said. "What do you want us to do?"

"I would like them to move two or three of their tepees to the valley and set them up close to where Smith's man saw you. Then I would like to have four or five of your warriors join you to watch for anyone coming into the valley through the narrow canyon. In fact, I would like you to stop them from coming into the valley. It shouldn't take very many warriors to stop them while they're in the narrow canyon. In the canyon there is no place for them to seek cover, yet you and your warriors will have plenty of cover, and will be shooting down on them."

"We can do that," Red Owl said.

"I will take most of the warriors with me. We will be hiding behind where the cabin and barn were burned. We will let those coming in from over the ridge go by us. We will then ambush them from behind and force them to retreat into the open valley. We will probably get the heaviest of the fighting. If the ones coming in through the canyon retreat, then you can come and join us."

"It is a good plan," Red Owl said. "We will get started."

"I will return to my mine and wait for you there."

With that said, Frank thanked the leaders for their help then returned to the valley. He began preparing himself for what was to surely come as soon as the weather improved.

It wasn't long before over a dozen Indians arrived at the mine. They had three tepees and a number of supplies. Frank noticed Red Owl had the bow he had given him slung over his shoulder. Red Owl instructed his warriors where they were to set up the tepees, then walked with Frank to where he was to place the warriors who were to be fighting with Frank. Frank and Red Owl followed the buffalo trail part way up the ridge then moved off to one side among some rocks and trees.

"This is where I plan to hide until Smith and his men have gone by. As soon as they approach the edge of the woods, we will attack them from behind forcing them out into the open valley. We will fight them from the cover of the trees, while they try to defend themselves in the open. The only cover they will have will be in the creek.

"You will keep the others bottled up in the narrow canyon preventing them from helping the others," Frank explained.

Red Owl thought about Frank's plan for a moment. He began to nod his head that he agreed with the plan.

"I will have my warriors set up the tepees and stay there. I will have them keep an eye out to make sure we see them before they see us."

"That would be good. I will spend the night among the rocks and trees so we can see them first."

"Good. I will get my people in position. Good luck," Red Owl said.

"Good luck to you, Red Owl, and good hunting."

Red Owl left Frank at the mine and took several of his warriors to set up the tepees and settle in for the night. It was getting on toward dark by the time Red Owl and his warriors got the tepees set up and prepared themselves for what was to come in the morning. The fog had started to clear as the sun set over the mountains to the west.

Frank took those warriors that were going to help him to where he had planned to hunker down for the night. They had good cover among the trees and rocks with a good escape route, if needed. With the plan to wait until Smith and his men had moved very close to the valley, Frank had the warriors relax with two of them keeping guard while the others rested, changing guards every two hours.

# CHAPTER TWENTY-FOUR

Frank woke before the sun was ready to come up. He looked around. Several of the warriors were still asleep and two were watching the buffalo trail where it came over the ridge. Frank was glad to see the fog had lifted and visibility was good. He rolled out of his bedroll and, being as quiet as possible, he moved over to where the warriors were sleeping. He gently woke each of them.

Using hand signals, he motioned them to remain quiet, then directed each of them to where he wanted them. When they were all in position, he settled in with them to wait. He was sure Smith would come over the ridge as soon as it was light enough for him to see the buffalo trail.

Time passed slowly with not a sound in the still morning air. As he looked at the warriors, Frank could see they were also patiently waiting for the fight to begin. Everyone was alert.

Suddenly, one of the warriors looked toward Frank and pointed toward the ridge. The warrior had obviously heard something. Frank motioned for the warriors to take cover. They had already been informed what the plan was, and they were ready to carry out the plan.

It wasn't long before Frank could hear the sound of horses' hooves on the hard ground. Slowly, the line of ranch hands moved past where Frank and the warriors were hiding. Frank could not see the riders except when they passed by a narrow opening in the rocks where Frank lay. Frank counted the number of riders. There were twelve riders, all well armed, and Smith. They patiently waited for them to go by.

As soon as Smith and his ranch hands had moved on past where Frank and the warriors were hiding, Frank motioned for the warriors to spread out on both sides of the trail, cutting off any possibility of their retreat back over the ridge. The closer Smith and his men got to the open valley, the closer Frank and the warriors moved in behind them.

Smith drew up at the edge of the woods and looked out into the valley. From his location he could see the three tepees near the lower end of the valley. It looked very quiet around the tepees.

"We'll wait here until Jesse comes up the canyon, then we'll attack the Indians from here. We'll have them trapped between us," Smith said with a slight grin.

"It looks pretty quiet down there. You think we caught 'um sleeping?" one of the ranch hands asked.

"I hope so, but keep an eye out. There may be more of them back in the woods."

"How long we gotta wait?" one of the ranch hands asked.

"Until Jesse starts the fight."

Time passed slowly as Smith and his men waited for the fight to begin. Some of the men were looking around, but they didn't see anything.

Frank could see Smith's men were getting nervous. It was very quiet, almost too quiet. Frank smiled to himself thinking that the quiet before a battle was almost as nerve racking as the sounds of the battle. He was sure that several of the ranch hands had never been in any kind of battle. They may have been in shootouts before, but nothing like a full scale battle.

Suddenly the peace and quiet of the mountain valley was broken by the sounds of gunfire. The horses Smith's men were riding suddenly high stepped and moved around nervously at the sounds of gunfire.

Frank gave the signal for the warriors to start shooting as Smith and his men charged out of the trees into the valley. The first volley of shots from the warriors took three men out of their saddles. It also caused several of the ranch hands to look back at the warriors. They turned and tried to defend themselves, but they were out in the open with no place to seek cover except along the creek. Three of the ranch hands tried to escape by riding as fast as they could for the other side of the valley and the safety of the trees, but only one of them made it to the trees, the other two were shot off their horses.

Frank saw Smith riding as fast as his horse would carry him toward the remains of the barn. It was the one place that would provide him with at least a little protection. Just as Smith was turning his horse toward where the barn had been, Frank fired a carefully aimed shot with his rifle. The bullet missed Smith, but struck his horse. The horse went down pinning Smith's leg to the ground under his dead horse. He yelled for help from his ranch hands, but they had enough troubles of their own.

The warriors had six of Smith's men pinned down in the creek. They were knee deep in icy water while lying as close to the bank of the stream as possible. The creek provided the only cover for them, and it wasn't much. To make a run for the woods would certainly mean their death.

The shooting at the lower end of the valley died down rather quickly. Red Owl led his warriors up along the edge of the woods on the opposite side of the valley from Frank. They captured the one ranch hand who had made it across the valley and into the woods.

With Red Owl and his warriors on one side of the valley and Frank with his warriors on the other side, they had the remaining ranch hands pinned down with no place to go. Only five of the six ranch hands who made to the creek were alive.

It wasn't long before the remaining ranch hands realized that to continue to fight would only end in their death, but the options were few. They could fight to their death while lying in the creek, or they could surrender and die at the hands of the Indians who were sure to torture them to death. Not much of a choice.

"Give it up," Frank called out to the few ranch hands that were left alive. "Give up or die right there."

"The Indians will torture us. We are better off to fight to the death," one of the ranch hands yelled back.

"They will not torture you if you drop your guns and come out with your hands in the air."

There was silence for several minutes. No one was shooting at them. It was clear that the man who had called to them was a white man.

"Who are you?" one of the ranch hands asked.

"Frank Griswold. I will turn you over to the law if you surrender now."

"I didn't know Griswold was around here," one of the ranch hands said to the others nearby.

"Tell me something," one of the other ranch hands called out. "Is Mrs. McDonald alive?"

"Yes. She is alive and well."

The ranch hand who asked about Mrs. McDonald looked at the others and said, "If we surrender, all they can get us for is burning down the cabin and barn, and trespassing."

"We'll end up hanging," another said.

"No. If we tell them what Smith has been doing, the worst will be a few years in jail. I'm willin' to do a few years in jail rather than die at the hands of those Indians or swing at the end of a rope," another said.

"Me, too," another said.

Those still alive in the creek agreed that prison was better than the gallows, and better than dying at the hands of the Indians. The cold water of the creek was starting to make their legs numb. It wouldn't be long before they would not be able to stand.

"I'm surrenderin'," one of the ranch hands said, then slowly stood up.

The ranch hand tossed his gun down on the ground at the edge of the creek then put his hands in the air. Since no one shot at him, he climbed out of the creek. As soon as the others saw that no one shot at him, they tossed out their guns and climbed out of the creek with their hands in the air.

"Is that all of you?" Frank called out.

"All but one, and he's dead," one of the ranch hands said.

"Okay. Walk toward me."

The five ranch hands began walking toward Frank. It wasn't long and they were surrounded by several Indians. Their faces showed they were afraid Frank might not have any control over the Indians, and they would be tortured even though Frank had assured them they would not be tortured.

Red Owl and his warriors came across the valley with the one ranch hand who had gotten to the woods. He walked up to the others that had given up.

"Red Owl, take them over to where the barn was and build a fire. We will get them warm and dry before we get them ready to take to Custer City and turn them over to white man's law."

Red Owl's warriors took them over near where the barn had been. They built a fire and allowed the ranch hands to get warm and dry while the Indians guarded them. As soon as they were warm, they were tied up.

Once their prisoners were secure, Frank and Red Owl walked over to where Smith's horse had fallen dead. They found that Smith's horse had fallen on his leg and trapped him under the horse, but Smith was still alive.

Red Owl took the bow from his shoulder and put an arrow in it. He drew back the arrow and pointed it at Smith.

"Don't do it, Red Owl. Let white man's law deal with him," Frank said.

"What will white man do to him?"

"I'm sure he will be found guilty of murdering Mrs. McDonald's husband, stealing her cattle and stealing her horses. He will hang for those things," Frank assured him.

"It is too bad he can't hang more than once," Red Owl said.

"I agree with you," Frank said with a grin.

Just then, one of Red Owl's warriors touched Red Owl on the shoulder and pointed toward the lower part of the valley. Red Owl looked where the warrior was pointing and saw three horses coming toward them.

"Frank," Red Owl said, then pointed toward the riders. Frank looked at where he was pointing and saw Susan and two other riders.

"It's okay. That's Mrs. McDonald and John Miller from the Four Mile Stage Stop, and Sheriff Metcalf, the county sheriff."

Frank and Red Owl watched as the three rode up to them. Susan looked around and saw Smith still pinned under his horse. She then turned and looked at Frank. As she got off her horse, she noticed that Smith was reaching for a gun.

"Frank," Susan yelled as she quickly drew her gun and shot at Smith.

Frank also shot at the same time. Both shots hit Smith. Susan's bullet hit him in the leg. Frank's bullet hit him in the shoulder causing him to drop the gun. Neither bullet would kill him. Red Owl quickly turned and had his bow drawn and an arrow pointed at Smith, but didn't let the arrow go.

As soon as they realized Smith was no longer a threat, Frank turned to Susan. She looked over at Frank then ran to him, put her arms around him and held him tight. She laid her head on Frank's chest and started to cry.

Sheriff Metcalf looked around at the prisoners and the dead, then shook his head. He turned and looked at Frank.

"It looks like you've had a bit of a fight on your hands," the sheriff said interrupting Frank and Susan's moment. "We saw three dead men in the narrow canyon coming into the valley."

"Yeah," Frank said as he held onto Susan and looked at the sheriff over her shoulder.

"There're two dead over on the other side of the valley close to the line of trees. There are three more dead out there in the open and another one in the creek," Frank said as he pointed to each location. "We also have six prisoners for you as well. Seven if you count Smith."

Just then two of Red Owl's warriors came out of the woods with one of Smith's ranch hands. He had given himself up when he saw the others give up.

"Why don't you take Mrs. McDonald someplace away from all this," the sheriff suggested. "We'll collect the bodies and horses, and take care of the prisoners."

"We will help," Red Owl said.

"Red Owl, come and get me when the sheriff is ready to head back to Custer City."

Red Owl nodded that he understood, then Frank turned and took Susan to the mine. The sheriff took charge of the prisoners with the help of a couple of Red Owl's warriors. Red Owl and the rest of his warriors gathered up all the dead men, their horses and weapons. Red Owl left the valley with the dead. He wasn't gone very long when he returned with the horses.

"Where are your warriors, Red Owl?" the sheriff asked.

"They are burying the dead as white men do. We took them out of the valley."

"Good. I'm sure Mrs. McDonald will be pleased about that."

Just then Frank rode up on his dapple gray horse. Frank stepped down and looked around.

"Red Owl, what are you going to do with the horses from the dead?" Frank asked.

"They belong to you," Red Owl replied.

"I think you might want to keep them. Consider them a gift for all your help. I will be going over to the Smith ranch and getting Mrs. McDonald's horses back for her."

"I understand that she has some cattle over there, too. You might as well get them, too," the sheriff suggested.

"I would like that, but it would be a little hard to care for them here right now."

"Since Smith had Mrs. McDonald's cabin and barn burned down, I think it's only fair that you use his barn and ranch house while you rebuild here in the valley. Besides, Smith isn't goin' to have much use for it. It will take a while to get everything settled and his next of kin notified of his death. Once you get this place rebuilt, you can bring Mrs. McDonald's cattle and horses back here."

"Does Smith have any kin folk?"

"Not that I know of, that's why it will take a while to find out if he does, and to notify them of his death on the gallows," Sheriff Metcalf said with a grin.

"I think I'll take my prisoners to Smith's ranch and put them up in the bunk house for tonight."

"You need any help with them?"

"I will help watch them," Red Owl volunteered.

"Red Owl will help me guard them," Sheriff Metcalf said to Frank. "I think you should go look after Mrs. McDonald. I have a feeling she won't be Mrs. McDonald very long."

"I sure hope not," Frank said with a slight grin.

Frank watched as Sheriff Metcalf gathered up his prisoners, put them on horses and headed for the Smith

Ranch. As soon as the sheriff and Red Owl left the valley with the prisoners, Frank headed for the mine.

Susan was waiting for him when he rode up. He had hardly gotten off his horse when she threw her arms around his neck and held onto him tightly as she kissed him. After a long kiss, Susan looked up at him.

"Wow," Frank said as he caught his breath. "I've got a question for you."

"What's that?"

"Will you marry me?"

"Yes, yes," she said as she held onto him and kissed him again.

# EPILOGUE

Susan and Frank moved into the Smith ranch house. They lived in Smith's ranch house during the rest of the winter, and while they built a new cabin and barn in the small mountain valley ranch. In the spring, they moved all the cattle, including the new calves that were born in the spring to the valley ranch.

In late May, Susan and Frank were married in Custer City shortly after Smith was tried, convicted and hung for cattle rustling, theft of her horses and the murder of Jacob McDonald.

During the time that Susan and Frank were staying in Smith's ranch house, the sheriff searched for relatives. Frank oversaw Smith's ranch with the help of several new ranch hands he hired. When it was clear Smith didn't have any relatives, Frank filed for the land that made up the Smith ranch, then took over the ranch including all the buildings and all the livestock. Susan and Frank renamed it the Griswold Ranch.

The small valley ranch became a place where they could pasture their cattle during the hot summers. It also became a place where Susan and Frank could go when they wanted to be alone for a little while.

Susan and Frank lived a long life together raising cattle and several children. When their children were old enough, they let them run the Griswold Ranch. Susan and Frank retired to the small valley ranch where they enjoyed the beautiful valley during their sunset years.

58814198R00118

Made in the USA
Charleston, SC
19 July 2016